D0209326

*Ask Amy Green*

# DANCING DAZE

*Ask Amy Green*

# DANCING DAZE

## SARAH WEBB

CANDLEWICK PRESS

For Yazmin de Barra and Anna Aldridge,
my brilliant Young Editors

Copyright © 2012 by Sarah Webb

First U.S. edition 2013

Library of Congress Catalog Card Number 2012947258

ISBN 978-0-7636-5583-9

13 14 15 16 17 18 BVG 10 9 8 7 6 5 4 3 2 1

Printed in Berryville, VA, U.S.A.

This book was typeset in ITC Giovanni.

Candlewick Press
99 Dover Street
Somerville, Massachusetts 02144

visit us at www.candlewick.com

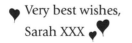

Hi! Welcome to *Dancing Daze*. This was a really fun book to write, as I'm a ballet nut and it gave me a brilliant excuse to talk to dancers and travel to the beautiful Opera House in Budapest to watch a ballet (swoon!) and to check out dance movies and shows. Even if you're not a dance fan like me, I hope you'll still enjoy reading about Claire Starr's journey from normal Irish schoolgirl to ballerina, with all its highs and lows, as told to her top secret diary. Lots of this story is set in Budapest, and if you ever get the chance to visit this magical city, go, go, go!

I'd be horrified if anyone got their sticky mitts on my diary! I've been writing one since I was a teenager. I have lots of them now, and I love plucking one from my *very secret and secure* hiding place (note to my family: no point looking, folks, believe me) and reading what I was up to on the very same day five, ten, or even twenty years ago.

Do you keep a diary? If not, it's never too late to start. And in twenty years' time, you might be able to read about all the mischief your teen self was up to, just like me!

♥ Very best wishes,
   Sarah XXX ♥

# ♥ Chapter 1

I'm in my best friend Mills's ultratidy bedroom when her mum, Sue, walks in, a huge grin on her face. "There's someone here who wants to speak to you," she says, handing the house phone to Mills.

"Hello?" Mills says into the receiver, and then her eyes light up. "Claire!" she squeals. "You haven't rung for ages and ages. How's your toe? Has the nail dropped off yet? Is there still loads of snow in Budapest?"

Claire is Mills's big sister, and she moved to Budapest when she was fifteen to study ballet at the Budapest Ballet Academy. She's now a soloist, and the company is dancing *Romeo and Juliet* in a big theater in Dublin just before Christmas, and Claire is playing Juliet! Dad's bank is sponsoring the event, so he's already booked us all tickets to see her.

"When will you be home for *Romeo and Juliet?*" Mills is asking now. (Claire may be a brilliant dancer, but she's hopeless at keeping in touch with her family, and I know Mills misses her horribly.)

Mills's eyes widen. "Holy Moly!" she shrieks, bouncing up and down on the bed with excitement. "That's brilliant news. And I can't believe you'll be on the telly." There's a pause. "Oh, OK. I'll tell Mum. Love you too!" Mills clicks the phone off and hands it back to Sue. "Claire said to say bye and that she'll e-mail you her flight details. Did you know about the publicity trip, Mum?"

Sue shakes her head. "I had no idea. Isn't it brilliant? I can't wait to see her. Now, Amy looks like she's about to explode with curiosity, so I'll leave you to tell her the news." She leans over and gives Mills a hug. "My two girls, back under the same roof." Her eyes water and she waves a hand in front of her face. "Sorry, I just miss her so much."

"Me too, Mum," Mills says.

Sue was right. I am dying to know the news, so as soon as she's out the door, I turn to Mills. "What's happening? Sounds pretty exciting."

"Claire's coming home next Thursday to do some preshow publicity for *Romeo and Juliet.* She'll be here for only a couple of days, but she's going to be on the

*Late Late Show* on Friday night with the Hungarian dancer who plays Romeo. She wants us to come to the airport to collect her. You too, if you like."

"No way!" I say. "That's fantastic. All the olds in Ireland watch that show. She's going to be mega-famous after it. And yes, please. I do love a good airport reunion. Count me in."

On the way to Dublin airport the following Thursday evening, Mills and I take one final look at *Ballet Barbie*, the book I helped Mills create for her sister. Mills wanted to make a special scrapbook to celebrate Claire's homecoming, and with my aunt Clover's assistance, I found this amazing website called makeabook.com. Clover knows everything about everything, and at eighteen, with her long white-blond hair, rock-star boyfriend, and job at the *Goss* teen magazine, she's the coolest aunt around.

The makeabook site allows you to pick a style, then scan in photos (and anything else you'd like to see on the pages), add text, and preview it carefully (checking for any spelling mistakes). You press "print"—and *voilà:* two days later, a rather fabulous one-of-a-kind book arrives in the post. (Clover very sweetly paid for the book on her credit card and refused to let Mills pay her back.)

Mills carefully opens the ballet-shoe-pink hard-cover. "'To Ballet Barbie, Lots and lots of love, Mills,'" she reads. "Ballet Barbie" is Mills's nickname for her big sis.

"'Chapter One,'" she continues. "'The Early Days. From the very beginning, Claire Starr was born to dance. Her mum, Sue, says Claire was bopping along to the radio as soon as she could stand. As a tiny tot, Claire especially loved dancing to the Spice Girls.'"

Sue laughs from the front passenger seat. "She certainly did. I used to call her 'Dancing Spice.'"

"That's true," Mills's dad agrees quietly. I like Allan Starr, but he is very, very normal. Some people may even call him boring. . . . I've only ever seen him in a checked shirt and beige chinos. Clover says the most exciting thing about him is the unusual spelling of his name.

Mills points to one of the photos in chapter one, an adorable image of Claire as a little girl wearing a tiny white tutu, both hands over her head, fingers touching, like a real ballerina.

"Already performing at three," Mills says.

I smile. "That's such a cute shot."

"She started at Miss Smitten's School of Dance just after that," Sue says. "By the time she was five, she insisted on going to two classes a week. Remember, Allan?"

Allan laughs heartily and slaps the steering wheel. "Do I ever. When I told her it was too expensive, she said it could be her birthday present *and* her Christmas present. I nearly fell off my chair. Imagine being that smart and determined at five!" He shakes his head. "But I guess all that determination has paid off."

We flick through the rest of the book: Claire, age six, dressed in rags as the Little Match Girl for one of her ballet school's shows; Claire, age eleven, doing an elegant arabesque in a plain pink cross-backed leotard.

We also added her ballet exam reports, all glowing, and some old cuttings from the Irish newspapers, including the front-page photograph of Claire in a full-length white tutu just after she'd been accepted at the Budapest Ballet Academy. Her dark brown eyes are staring proud and strong at the camera.

After we've studied the final page, an *Irish Times* piece about her upcoming starring role as Juliet in Dublin that calls her the "Irish Ballerina," Mills closes the book carefully and runs her hands over the front cover. "Do you think she'll like it?" she asks, biting her lower lip nervously.

"She'll adore it," I say. "I promise."

Mills smiles at me gratefully. She seems mega-nervous about seeing Claire again. Claire's been home only once since she left for Budapest two years ago, and I know Mills and her parents find it hard to see her so rarely. Sue and Allan weren't at all keen on her going in the first place, but Claire dug her heels in. She was determined to go, and that was that.

As soon as we get to Dublin airport, Allan heads for the huge flight-information board with its flickering yellow numbers and letters. He sighs. "Sheesh, that's just typical. Delayed by twenty minutes. The parking's going to cost me a fortune."

Sue pats his arm. "Not to worry, dear. Let's get a coffee and then we can all wait in the arrivals area. It won't be long now."

Mills and I have a mooch around the shop, checking out the magazines, before joining the older Starrs again. Sue has brought her knitting and is clicking away while Mr. Starr sits slumped in his seat, his arms crossed, scowling up at the arrivals board.

Our bums are almost numb from the plastic seats when Mills jumps to her feet half an hour later. "There she is, Ames. It's Claire! Look!" She grabs my arm and pulls me toward the metal barrier to greet her.

Claire is bumping shoulders with a boy who looks about nineteen or twenty years old. He has a mop of dark-blond curly hair, chestnut eyes, full, pouty lips, and the cheekiest expression I've ever seen. He must be the boy playing Romeo. Lucky Claire!

"Claire!" Mills waves her arm frantically at her sister. "Over here."

Claire's head whips around. She looks different from how I remember her — taller and more angular. Her face is definitely thinner. Her cheekbones are more pronounced, making her stunning eyes look like two huge pools of chocolate. Her hair is pulled back into a high, swishy ponytail, and she's wearing a pearl-gray crewneck sweater, black-leather jacket, black skinny jeans, and black biker boots. She looks impossibly cool, like a movie star.

Claire beams at Mills, drops her silver wheelie bag at her feet, and runs toward her sister. She swings herself over the barrier and throws herself into Mills's arms.

"Mills!" she says, jumping up and down on the spot and hugging her close. "It's so good to see you. I've missed you so much, baby sis."

"I've missed you too." Mills's eyes are sparkling with happy tears, and from the wobble in her voice, I can tell she's choking up.

Claire puts her hands on Mills's shoulders and takes a good look at her. She sighs and shakes her head. "Look at you, all grown up. You look amazing. That boyfriend you've been telling me about in your e-mails is one lucky boy."

Mills's cheeks go pink. "Claire! Stop embarrassing me."

"Embarrassing you is my job, sis. And hiya, Amy." Claire smiles at me. "Good to see you. . . . And there you are, Mum," she says to Sue, who has been waiting patiently beside Mills. "Looking gorgeous, as always." Claire gives her mum a warm hug.

"Gosh, you're very bony," Sue says as she draws away. She touches Claire's cheek. "Have you been eating enough? Are you taking those supplements I sent over? And you look a little . . . tired. Is everything all right?"

For a second a shadow passes over Claire's face. Then she says, "Stop fretting, Mum. I've only just got here." She smiles again. "I know you're dying to feed me, and I can't wait. I've seriously missed your cooking. And Dad. Hello." She gives him a hug too. "Thanks for coming to collect me."

"My pleasure, pet," Allan says. "We're all delighted to have you home. But I think you may be forgetting something. Or someone." He nods at Romeo.

"Oh, that's Péter, my dance partner," Claire explains. She pronounces the name with a lilt in the middle — P-*eh*-ter — and for a second, she sounds more Hungarian than Irish. "I told you about him, right?"

"Isn't he your Romeo?" Mills asks, wiggling her eyebrows.

Claire goes a little red. "Yes. But it's not like that, believe me. Can we give him a lift to the Merrion Hotel, Dad? That's where we're staying."

Mills's face drops. "I thought you were staying with us."

Claire shrugs. "I'm sorry. It's all been set up by the theater's PR people over here. We have a packed schedule. It's booked solid with interviews and photo shoots to promote the show in December. I'm here for three nights only. I'm sorry. I thought you knew, sis . . ." She trails off and looks at Sue. "Didn't you tell her, Mum? I'm sure I put it in the e-mail. Maybe I didn't. I have a lot on my mind and sometimes I forget things."

Mr. Starr pats Claire's shoulder. "Don't you worry, pet, you didn't forget, but I rang the theater's publicity department and sorted it all out. They said that of course you should stay with your family. You have a photo shoot at the theater in the morning, followed by some interviews, so they're going to send a taxi over to collect you from home at nine. But they don't need you in the afternoon, so if we can get you to RTÉ for the *Late Late Show* rehearsal by seven, you're all ours for a while. Your mum and I thought we could do something together as a family tomorrow. Maybe go for a walk up Killiney Hill and have an early dinner in Dalkey. Plus, the theater's publicity manager has arranged two tickets to the telly show for us. Isn't that great? Sadly, she wasn't able to get a third one for Mills, but she and Amy are going to watch it at home."

"I'm not sure you should have done that, Dad," Claire says.

"What?" Allan looks flabbergasted.

"Ringing the PR department like that is a bit unprofessional. This is my *career*, and I don't want everyone back in Budapest thinking I'm some sort of soft Irish girl who has to go home to her mummy and daddy for some home cooking and hugs whenever she's in Dublin."

"Claire Starr, your dad meant well," Sue says, looking taken aback. "He didn't mean to annoy you. And it was my idea to ring the PR manager, so I think you owe him an apology." Her voice softens. "I know your career means the world to you, but we've all missed you, pet, very much. And any time we can spend with you is very precious. We'd love you to stay at home with us, but if you can't, you can't. We understand, don't we, Allan?"

Allan nods but doesn't say anything. Mills is biting down so hard on her lip that it's almost white.

Claire notices Mills's expression and backs down immediately. "I'm sorry, Dad, OK? I didn't mean to snap at you. I'm just wiped out from traveling. And I've missed you all too. I'd love to stay at home."

"Good. Thank you, darling," Sue says with a relieved smile. "That's all settled, then."

Péter is still waiting patiently on the far side of the barrier. "Apologies, Péter," Claire says, calling him over. He makes his way toward us, pulling Claire's wheelie bag behind him like a puppy. His own bag is slung over one of his strong-looking shoulders.

"I was just sorting something out with my family," Claire explains. "Dad's going to drop you at your hotel, but I'm going to stay at home. This is Péter Bako, everyone, one of the best dancers in Hungary."

"*The* best dancer in Hungary," Péter says, correcting Claire in perfect English. "Charmed to meet you all."

The awkward atmosphere lifts as he grins and gives a flamboyant bow. And, boy, is he good-looking up close and personal.

He chats away easily to Allan and Sue about the flight. Mills nudges me in the side. "Wowzers!" she whispers, fanning her face with her hand.

"No kidding," I whisper back. "Who knew ballet boys were so hot?" I smile at her. "Happy?"

She nods eagerly. "Very. And I can't wait to give Claire her book. I think I'll wait until tomorrow afternoon, when she isn't so exhausted."

Then she hooks my arm with hers and we follow the Starr family and Péter out of the arrivals hall and toward the car park, trying very hard not to stare at Péter's perfectly formed bum.

# ♥ Chapter 2

"Amy, I think there's something wrong with Claire."
Mills shifts around uneasily on the couch. It's Friday
night and I've just gotten to her house. We're waiting
to watch Claire's *Late Late Show* appearance together.

"Why do you say that?" I ask.

"Well, we were supposed to be going for a walk
up Killiney Hill this afternoon, but she said she was
too tired. And she didn't want to go out for dinner
tonight either. Said she wasn't hungry and asked Mum
to make her something to eat in her room instead."

"She flew back only last night, Mills," I say gently.
(Mills does tend to overreact sometimes.) "Maybe she's
just exhausted and nervous about the *Late Late Show.*"

"It's more than that. She just had some coffee
and toast for breakfast this morning, even though

Mum had made pancakes. Usually she wolfs down Mum's food. She has a huge appetite. Says she needs extra fuel for all her dance practice. She isn't sleeping either. Last night I woke up at three and heard a noise coming from her room, so I went in to check that she was all right, and she was wide awake. I asked her if everything was OK, and she admitted that she's seriously worried about dancing Juliet in front of a home crowd. It's her first big role, you see, and she wants it to be perfect. She thinks that's what's keeping her awake."

Ah, the Starr perfection curse.

"That would explain the insomnia, all right," I say. "Most performers get nervous before important shows, though. I'm sure it's perfectly normal."

"I guess."

"You don't sound convinced."

Mills pauses. "Look, Ames, I swore I'd keep it to myself, but this afternoon, after I gave Claire the scrapbook and we looked through it together — she loved it, by the way, especially all the old photos — she said, 'Be careful what you wish for, eh?' Then she told me about all the hours of ballet practice she has to do every day — and it sounds pretty grueling — and then she started to *cry*. She tried to cover it up by saying she was still out of whack from the flight and that was why her eyes kept watering, but they were definitely tears."

Claire Starr, crying about dance practice? That doesn't sound right. She's always been such a tough nut, taking pride in showing us her broken toenails and bruised feet from spending so much time in her pointe shoes.

Mills looks stricken. "I don't know what to do, Ames. If I tell Mum and Dad, they might stop her from dancing or something, and that would destroy her. I just want her to be happy again."

"Maybe it was just a blip," I suggest. "I'm sure she'll bounce back. This is Claire we're talking about, right? Miss Tough As Nails. Let's watch the show, and if you think she's acting strangely or out of character in any way, then we'll do something about it. Maybe we can ask Clover for help and come up with a plan. If Claire's back to her old sparkling self on the telly and you're not worried about her anymore, we won't. Does that make sense?"

"Perfect sense." Mills sighs happily. "You always know the right thing to do, Amy Green. I do love being your best friend."

I smile to myself. Mills really is a sweetie. "Thanks, Mills. Love you too, babes. Now, who else is on the *Late Late*, do you know?" I'm hoping to change the subject and cheer her up a bit. I check my watch. "It's on any minute now. Anyone famous? Johnny Depp?"

"You wish." She laughs. "Billy Brady from Coast is on just before Claire and Péter." She clutches her heart and makes a funny little *squee* noise that makes me smile. (Coast is a new Irish boy band, a younger version of Westlife, and their lead singer, Billy Brady, looks like Zac Efron. I'm not really a fan — their music is too vanilla for me — but Mills is right. Billy's cute.)

The show's opening credits start rolling, and Mills turns up the sound so loud that the theme song blasts out, making my ears ring.

"Mills! Are you trying to deafen me?"

"Sorry." She lowers the volume.

"Welcome to the *Late Late Show*," the presenter, Renee O'Reilly, a tall blond woman with huge green eyes, says. "And do we have a show for you tonight. Coming up in a moment we have Claire Starr, the Irish Ballerina, and her dance partner and Romeo, Péter Bako."

Mills grabs my arm in excitement and squeals. "Yeah!"

"We also have the California relationship guru they call the Heart Whisperer," Renee continues, "and a brilliant sketch from the Comedy Chicks. But first, to kick off the show, the latest single from Coast . . ."

The women in the audience whistle and cheer.

"Easy, ladies," Renee says with a smile. "We'll be having a chat with the boys later, so stay tuned for that too."

As the band walk onto the set, wearing identical dark-blue suits, and start singing, I switch off a little, but Mills is swaying to the music, a goofy grin on her face. I look around the room, and my eyes rest on the mantelpiece. It's decorated with framed family photographs, mostly of Mills and Claire together: toddler Mills and a mini version of Claire wearing Santa hats; Mills and Claire, at about four and eight, wearing matching pink skiing suits; Mills and Claire and Mickey Mouse — both sisters squinting in the sun — taken at Disney World; a larger professional-looking photograph taken when Claire was about our age of her looking stunning and elegant in a pale-blue-and-silver tutu, balancing on one pointe, with blue feathers in her scraped-back hair.

When Coast have finished singing and soaking up their applause, they leave the set. I concentrate on the screen again.

"Wasn't that wonderful?" Renee says. "Now I'd like you to please give a very warm welcome to the Irish Ballerina, Claire Starr, and her Hungarian Romeo, Péter Bako."

Claire strides through an archway toward Renee in a stunning full-length, swishy silver evening dress. She is followed by Péter, who's wearing tight black trousers and a snug-fitting white shirt unbuttoned almost to his belly button. Either Claire is no longer nervous or she's a great actor. She looks poised and confident but incredibly thin. Her neck is all muscles and sinews, like a racehorse's, and there is so little fat on her that you can see her ribs and hip bones through her dress. But then, maybe all dancers have ultratoned bodies. Péter is lean too.

"Holy Moly, there she is," Mills shrieks, jumping up and down on the sofa and clapping her hands together. "My sis, on the *Late Late Show*."

"We're delighted to have you on the show, Péter and Claire," Renee says. "Or should I call you Romeo and Juliet?"

They both smile at her, but Claire's smile doesn't quite reach her eyes. "Péter and Claire is just fine," she says.

"They look great together, don't they?" I say, nudging Mills with my elbow. "Do you think they're a couple? Did Claire say anything about it?"

"Shush!" Mills hisses at me. She grabs the remote

and turns up the volume again. "Stop talking, I'll miss something."

"Sorry," I say a little huffily. "I was just wondering."

"Now, Claire and Péter," Renee says. "You're dancing the lead roles in *Romeo and Juliet*, which opens in the Bord Gáis Energy Theatre on December twenty-first. Claire, tell us how your version of the ballet is different from previous ones."

Is it my imagination or did Claire just gulp? Her eyes are flitting around the studio and not focusing on Renee's face. I think her nerves are starting to kick in!

"Say something," I will her.

"Go on, Claire," Mills adds, nibbling her lip.

Péter is looking at Claire, also wondering if she's going to answer Renee's question. But Claire still hasn't said a word. The question has clearly thrown her.

"Let's start with you, Péter," Renee says, taking control. Clutching her hands to her chest, she puts on a weird-sounding warbling voice: "'O Romeo, Romeo! Wherefore art thou Romeo? Deny thy father and refuse thy name. Or, if thou wilt not, be but sworn my love, And I'll no longer be a Capulet.'" Renee beams at him, clearly delighted with herself.

As the audience claps politely, Péter looks at Claire and gives a tiny roll of his eyes. Claire smiles a little. Luckily Renee is staring straight into the camera and doesn't notice. "My darling lady," Péter says, turning to Renee. "I have never before heard that quotation spoken quite so beautifully."

Renee beams at him. "Why, thank you."

"What a lick," I murmur, and Mills shushes me again.

"I will answer your question," Péter continues. "My Romeo is as Shakespeare intended: young, foolhardy, desperately in love." He slides forward in his chair, and waves his arms around wildly. "Our version is all about love. Love, love, love. And passion. And desire. I dance with all my heart. I jump, I spin, I tumble, but it is here"—he runs a hand down his face—"here that matters. My expression. My face. I want the audience to feel what Romeo feels inside." He hits his chest with a closed fist. "For two hours, I want them to live through what Romeo lives through. When his heart breaks, I want their hearts to break. And that is what makes my Romeo different." He sits back and crosses his arms.

Renee looks a little taken aback by his passionate response, but she recovers quickly. "And a lovely face it is too," she says. "And can I come to you now, Claire?

There are rumors that you and Péter are, in fact, an item. Are they true?"

Mills gives a squeak and turns the telly up even louder.

Péter is grinning from ear to ear, his eyes fixed on Claire's face. Claire says nothing for a few seconds, her cheeks blushing again. Then, with what seems like an enormous effort, the edges of her mouth lift. "That would be . . . telling," she says, faltering, before continuing with more confidence. "You'll just have to see the show and decide for yourself, Renee."

Mills gasps. "Maybe they are in love."

I'm not convinced. Claire's answer sounded too practiced, as if her PR woman had told her what to say.

The show goes to an ad break then, so instead of disagreeing with Mills (after all, it's not every night your sister is on the telly), I say, "Claire looks amazing. Is that slinky dress hers?"

"Unfortunately, no. They found it for her in the RTÉ costume department. Claire thought she was dancing on the show, not talking, so she had nothing to wear."

My mobile beeps twice and I check my messages. One's from Mum: HOME STRAIGHT AFTER CLAIRE'S SLOT—ISN'T SHE DOING WELL? MUM XXX

The second's from Seth: SORRY I WON'T GET TO SEE YOU THIS WEEKEND. YOU'RE AT YOUR DAD'S, RIGHT? AND I'M BEING THE PHOTOGRAPHER'S ASSISTANT AT A 60TH BIRTHDAY PARTY SATURDAY, AND A CHRISTENING ON SUNDAY, YAWN. SEE YOU IN SCHOOL. MISS YOU ALREADY, SETH X

Seth's my boyfriend, and he often helps his mum (he calls her Polly) on the weekends. She's a photographer. There's only the two of them, and they're very close. Bailey, Mills's boyfriend, is Seth's best friend, but they're very different. Seth is blond and easygoing. Bailey's dark-haired and more complicated, but he's utterly devoted to Mills.

"Anything interesting?" Mills asks, twisting her neck to try to read my screen. "Oh, Seth. *'Miss you already.'* Isn't that sweet? I do adore Seth. He's such a cutie."

She watches as I tap in a simple SEE YOU THEN. MISS YOU TOO. AMY. BIG X, and press "send."

"Is that it?" she asks. "That's all you're sending him? One *x*."

"A big *x*," I protest. "Why? What would you suggest, O Love Text Guru?"

"Bailey's always sending me lines of corny old love songs." Mills and Bailey have officially been together since October, but it feels like forever. And not always in a good way.

"Sounds scintillating," I say.

"Don't be so snarky, Ames. At least it's inventive. And I send him poetry sometimes."

"Poetry? Seriously? What kind of poetry?" I put on a posh theatrical voice and throw an arm out in front of me. "'My luuuurve is like a red, red rose.' That kind of thing?"

She scowls. "Are you making fun of me, Amy Green?"

I pretend to look shocked. "Of course not, Amelia Starr. But I think Seth would split his sides laughing if I started spouting text poetry at him. We're not gushy like that." (I don't tell her that Seth does, in fact, write me poetry from time to time. It's personal, and he'd kill me if I ever told anyone, especially Mills. Some things should be kept private.)

After a beat, she says, "OK, I get it," rather too knowingly for my liking.

"What does that mean?"

"The spark has clearly gone out of your relationship, that's all. You're like an old married couple."

"We are not. That's a criminal thing to say, Mills."

She puts a hand up like a traffic cop. "Shush. The show's back."

Renee starts asking Claire about her background and training, and I tune out. I'm still fuming about Mills's old-married-couple gibe. How dare she? Now that Mills has Bailey, she thinks she's the world's expert on relationships and boys. It's most aggravating. I've been with Seth way longer than she's been with Bailey. And it's not as if they haven't had their problems. Bailey even cheated on Mills a while back, and Seth would never do something like that. Bailey was going through a really rough time at home, but it was still a horrible thing to do. So Mills is hardly the right person to give me relationship advice.

"Amy?" Mills says. "Did you hear that? Claire just thanked her family for supporting her over the years, and her old dance teacher, Miss Smitten. Isn't that sweet?"

"Yes," I say, tuning back in to the show. I'm supposed to be watching Claire's performance for signs of stress, not obsessing about my own life. Concentrate, Amy!

"How do you cope with being away from your family so much, Claire?" Renee asks. "You left home at fifteen to attend the Budapest Ballet Academy, is that right? It's very young."

"It is young," Claire agrees, her face serious. "Maybe a little too young, but it was a once-in-a-lifetime opportunity. All I've ever wanted to do is dance. It was my dream." She shrugs. "But I don't think I realized how hard I would have to work to be accepted. And I was terribly homesick at first. I still miss my family, and especially my little sister, Mills. Hi, Mills, if you're watching." Claire smiles at the camera, her first genuine smile of the whole interview.

"Hi, Claire," Mills says excitedly, waving at the screen.

I laugh. "Don't think she can hear you."

"She said my name on the telly. I'm famous." Mills falls back against the sofa and sighs dreamily.

Renee leans forward in her chair. "And Claire, Péter, does either of you get nervous before a big show like *Romeo and Juliet*? They're huge roles, and it's a lot to take on."

Péter shrugs. "A little, but not much, and once I've stepped onto the stage, the nerves, they go away. For Claire, I think it is worse, yes?" He looks at Claire, his eyes soft, and she lifts her head — she's been staring down at her hands — and nods.

"I get terrible stage fright," she admits. "My hands shake and I can't keep anything down for hours before a performance. But, like Péter, once I'm onstage, I'm OK. It's just thinking about everything beforehand that gets to me, you know? Worrying that I'll make stupid mistakes and let myself and the company down. I'm the only Irish dancer in the Dublin show and I know people will be coming to see me — the 'Irish Ballerina.'" She pauses, as if slightly overwhelmed by the thought, and then takes a deep breath. "It's a huge responsibility. I want everyone to be proud of me, especially my family."

I try to imagine what it must be like to carry an entire megaballet production on your shoulders. *Yikes!* No wonder Claire feels under pressure.

"It is a huge responsibility," Renee agrees. "But I'm sure you'll do both yourself and your company proud. Isn't that right, Péter?"

"Yes," he says strongly, turning his whole body toward Claire. "You will be a wonderful, beautiful Juliet. I know this with my heart." He takes her hand and kisses it softly. "And I will be right beside you on that stage, cheering you on with my whole being."

Claire's eyes are sparkling in the lights. Is she crying? She blinks several times and mouths, "Thank you," at him. It seems like a very sweet, private moment, and Mills and I both say, *"Aaaahh,"* and smile at each other.

"If you don't mind my saying, you both seem very mature for your ages," Renee says. "Claire, you are seventeen, Péter, nineteen. Is that right?"

They both nod.

Renee tilts her head. "Do professional dancers ever go wild like normal teenagers, break out a little? Do you go clubbing with your Hungarian ballet friends, Claire? You guys must tear up the dance floor, am I right?"

Claire looks upset and then, clearly aware that Renee is still looking at her, expecting an answer, says quietly, "I don't have much time for that kind of thing."

Péter jumps in. "Maybe you will take me dancing in Dublin, Claire, yes?"

Claire smiles and nods at him, but she still seems unhappy. As Renee is asking Péter about his training regime, inviting him to unbutton his shirt more and show the audience his abs—which he does slowly, with a cheeky grin, much to the delight and whoops of the audience—Claire sits right back in her seat, as if she'd like to sink into the leather and disappear. She's scratching one of her thumbs with a fingernail, and her mouth is set in a rigid line.

I'm sure most people are watching the animated conversation between the presenter and Péter, like

Mills is, but I'm studying Claire. She's blinking quickly and looks like she's about to cry. Renee's question about what she does for fun seems to have triggered something.

By the end of the interview, Claire has recovered a little, and her hands are still. But when Renee thanks her and Péter for coming on the show and wishes them luck in *Romeo and Juliet*, she looks heartily relieved that the interview is over.

As the show goes to another ad break, Mills claps her hands and grins. "Wasn't that amazing?" she gushes. "Apart from that silence after the first question, which I'm sure was just nerves, Claire rocked that interview. She's definitely back to her old self, which is a megarelief. She was smiling and joking around with Péter, who is a total babe, by the way. But, poor thing, I had no idea she gets such bad stage fright. Throwing up and everything must be horrible. No wonder she's not eating. I wouldn't either if I thought I was going to throw up all the time."

Mills seems oblivious of her sister's distress toward the end of the interview, and before I get the chance to say anything, her mobile rings. "It's Claire!" she says, answering it. "Hi, sis, you were fantastic, brilliant. . . . No, honest. . . . I'm not surprised you were nervous. She asked some pretty tough questions. . . . You met

Coast in the greenroom? I'm so jealous. What's Billy like in person? . . . They're doing a concert really? When?" Mills chatters on excitedly.

Claire's reaction to Renee's last question is still niggling at me. Something isn't right. Why would Claire react so badly to being asked what she does for fun? It's weird.

"OK, talk to you later. Enjoy the rest of the show." Mills clicks off her mobile and grins at me. "Claire says Billy is dreamy in real life, and at the end of the show, Coast will announce the dates for their new concert tour. They've just been uploaded onto their website, apparently. Let's go on Claire's laptop and have a look. It's really fast to boot up. Not like Dad's old thing. I think it's in her room."

Still mulling over what could be up with Claire, I follow Mills upstairs.

Claire's room, the largest bedroom in the house, is like a time capsule. It's exactly the way it was when she left for Budapest two years ago, right down to the posters on the wall and the pink-and-white-ballerina curtains that Sue made when Claire was little. Mills used to have cute brown-and-yellow-cowgirl curtains, but she asked Sue to change them years ago. Claire loved hers so much, though, that she kept them, even as a teenager.

The whole room is a shrine to ballet, but it's always looked a bit bare. The floor is covered in cork tiles, and, apart from the bed pressed up against the left-hand wall and the built-in wardrobe, there isn't any other furniture, not even a desk. But there's a reason for this: it used to double up as Claire's own private dance studio. There's a wooden barre along the right-hand wall in front of a floor-to-ceiling mirror, where Claire used to practice. Both were made from scratch and put in place by Allan Starr, who's a real Handy Andy (unlike like my dad, who can barely change a lightbulb).

Posters and photographs of famous ballerinas — Margot Fonteyn, Darcey Bussell, and Olga Varga, the most famous Hungarian ballerina ever — stare down from the other three walls. They are all wearing fluffy white tutus and balancing on their tippy-toes while doing impossible-looking bendy things with their legs. Claire admires them all, but Olga is her idol. Her voice goes all hushed whenever she says Olga's name, as if she is some sort of saint or something.

The room is as neat as Mills's, apart from the bed, which is heaped with a muddle of tops and jeans, a hair dryer, a huge silver makeup bag the size of my schoolbag, two pairs of slightly grubby-looking pointe shoes, a black leotard, and a pair of balled-up off-pink ballet tights. Claire's silver hard-shell suitcase is almost hidden under the mess. And on top of the chaotic mountain is her small ultrathin black laptop. It's open, and the screen flickers brightly back to life as soon as Mills picks the laptop up.

"Here we are," she says. She clicks on Google and types in "Coast concert dates." "Claire was right. They are playing in January. Will you go with me, Ames, pretty please? Maybe we could bully Clover into taking us. Mum would never let me go without an adult, and Clover just about counts."

"I'll think about it." To be honest, I'd prefer not to, but Mills is my best friend. And we have to suffer for our besties! I'm sure Clover wouldn't mind. She's mad about any kind of music.

"Maybe Claire will come too," Mills says. "Maybe she could take a weekend off or something."

I look at Mills in surprise. Hasn't she been listening to a word her sister has been saying? Ballerinas don't seem to get much time off. Claire practically admitted that she doesn't have time for fun. But once again, Mills is lost in her own little world of unicorns and rainbows and totally oblivious of the people around her.

"I wonder if the *Late Late* clip is up on YouTube yet," she says. "I can't wait to put it up on my Facebook page. Annabelle will be so jealous. Me, mentioned on the telly!" (Annabelle's one of the mean girls at our school, Saint John's.)

As Mills clicks on YouTube, the battery icon comes up on the laptop screen. "The battery's dying," she says. "Claire must have left the power cord downstairs. She was showing Dad some new video clips of her dancing earlier. I'll be back in a second."

After Mills has gone, I check out Claire's snazzy laptop and notice a file saved on the desktop labeled "Budapest D." (D stands for dancing, I'm guessing.) Thinking it must be the clips that Claire was showing her dad earlier, I open it. But it's not a video file at all. It's a text file called "Budapest Diary." Curious, I click on it and start reading. The entry is dated yesterday.

Dear Diary,

It's so weird being home again. Everything looks the same and yet different, like I'm looking at the world through special "visitor" glasses. My bedroom is just as I left it, but it seems smaller. Did I really do my barre exercises in such cramped conditions? Still, Dad was sweet to build it, and I can't believe it's all still intact.

I can't settle. I feel like I don't belong here anymore. And with all the trouble back in Budapest, I don't feel like I belong there either. I'm in limbo, caught between two worlds and not comfortable in either.

I haven't slept a full night in weeks, with all the worry. I can't keep food down, and if I can't eat, I'm not going to have the energy to dance. And the whole company is relying on me to fill the seats in the Bord Gáis Energy Theatre, and that theater's huge! It's so much pressure, pressure, pressure. Péter says I should focus on getting the steps right instead of worrying about things I can't control.

I don't know what I'd do without Péter. He's the only reason I'm still in the company. If it wasn't for him, I couldn't bear it; I'd have to leave Budapest . . .

"Amy, I can't find the cord, but can I get you some OJ while I'm down here?" Mills shouts up the stairs.

I jump, only just grabbing the laptop before it crashes to the floor. I yell back, "Great, thanks," my heart racing. I feel horribly guilty about reading Claire's private thoughts, but from the sound of things, she really is in trouble. And what if it's serious?

The battery icon flashes again. I quickly take my keys out of my pocket, and before I've thought it through properly, I stick the memory stick I carry on my key ring into the USB port and copy the whole "Budapest D" file. I have no idea what I'm going to do with it, if anything, but something tells me I might just need it. As soon as I've copied it, the computer dies. Phew, just in time!

A few minutes later, Mills walks back into Claire's room, holding two large glasses of orange juice.

"The battery went, I'm afraid," I tell her.

She hands me a glass and sits down beside me on Claire's bed. "That's annoying, but never mind. I can pull the clip up in the morning. It's probably not on YouTube yet anyway." She takes a long drink of her juice.

"Don't you want to go back downstairs?" I ask her.

She shakes her head. "I like hanging out in here. I can smell Claire's perfume." She picks up a scarf and sniffs it.

"Mills, that's a bit weird."

"I know, but it makes me feel closer to her. She's flying back to Budapest on Sunday." She shrugs.

"How do you feel now?" I ask carefully. "After the telly interview, I mean. Are you still worried about her?"

I'm hoping she'll say yes, as somehow then I won't feel so bad about reading Claire's diary. But as I kind of suspected, she says, "No, I think Claire's fine. It's just bad stage fright. I can't wait to see her again at Christmas. And I still can't believe she was on the *Late Late Show.*"

She looks so idyllically happy that I can't bear to burst her bubble, so I nod wordlessly and drink my orange juice. And then as Mills starts talking about what she's going to wear to the Coast concert—next month!—I zone out, my mind mulling over Claire's Budapest "trouble." Maybe I'm overanalyzing things; it wouldn't be the first time. Maybe Mills is right that it is just bad nerves. After all, Mills knows her own sister, doesn't she?

When I get back to my house half an hour later, I take out my keys to open the front door, and my eyes linger on my memory stick. Claire's diary. And then I remember how my own diary used to help me make sense of my feelings and get things that were troubling me out of my system.

Recently its pages have been sadly neglected and not due to any lack of drama in my life, because, boy, do I have plenty to write about! No, I've just been too lazy to jot it all down. And I'd be truly horrified to discover that someone had read my diary, especially my little sister's friend.

I make two decisions: one, to delete Claire's file;

and two, to write in my diary at least once a week from now on. I'll make a start tonight and then do some more at Dad's house tomorrow. I'm often bored there, and it will give me something positive to do.

As I walk up to my bedroom, I wiggle the memory stick off the key ring. Then I put it in my desk drawer for safekeeping. I'll delete Claire's file later. After that, I find my diary, which is hidden behind some books on one of my bookshelves, grab a pen, sit on my bed, and start to write.

Friday, November 30

Dear Diary,
I'm sorry for neglecting you for ages and ages.
I do solemnly swear on Shakespeare's quill that
from now on I will write on your hallowed pages
at least once a week . . .

# ♥ Chapter 3

"I'm not sure I'm cut out for family life," Dad says as he drives away from my house on Saturday morning. "Shelly's sending me up the wall with her moaning, Gracie won't stop crying, and if Pauline Lame makes one more snide comment about the amount of golf I play, I swear I'll decapitate her with one of my putters. It's not natural, sharing a house with your mother-in-law."

Pauline Lame is Shelly's mum, and she's even scarier than my dad's new wife, Shelly, if that's possible. They look almost identical. They both have huge piano-key teeth, orange skin (from dodgy makeup layered on top of the fake tan), and billowing bleach-blond hair. They're like scary grown-up versions of the D4s in school, who wear Ugg boots and lather themselves in Oompa-Loompa-colored Fake Bake and dye their hair blond and say "OMG!" all the time.

"Plus, I'm afraid to go near my own wife for a kiss or a cuddle in case Pauline tut-tuts at me," Dad adds.

I wrinkle my nose. "Dad! I do not want to know!"

We pass the cluster of shops at the top of the hill and turn left instead of right.

"Where are we going?" I ask. "This isn't the way to your house."

"I'm dropping you off at Dundrum Shopping Centre. I have a few errands to run. Work stuff. You can have a bit of a shop and I'll collect you later. I know how you love Dundrum."

That sounds very suspicious. Dad's never had "errands" before. He's not the errands type. I happen to know his assistant, Agatha, buys all my birthday and Christmas presents. She has pretty good taste, so I don't really mind. Now, when Shelly was his assistant, the presents were rank.

"How long will you be?" I ask.

"A couple of hours tops. I'll ring you when I've finished my round — I mean, errands."

Suddenly, I know exactly what he's up to. Golf!

I turn around in my seat. Sure enough, his muddy black-and-white-leather golf shoes are sitting in one of the seat wells. "Dad, you swore to Shelly that you wouldn't play golf this Saturday. No wonder she's moaning at you. She has every right to get mad at you for breaking your promise."

"If I don't play a few quick holes, I'll explode, Amy. You don't understand the pressure I'm under at home. It's like being stuck on a medieval rack, with Shelly pulling my arms and Pauline stretching my legs. I can't win with those two. No, it's the golf course or the shrink's office. At least this way I'll get some fresh air."

"Is it really that bad?"

"Yes! It's appalling. Pauline is out of control. She can't sit still for one minute. She's got it into her head that the whole house needs to be redecorated. She says the hall has scuff marks from Gracie's buggy and that if she's going to invite friends around, the place needs to look decent. There are fabric swatches and paint charts on every surface, and she's already been testing colors on some of the walls. The hall's pockmarked with different shades of red. I don't like red, and it's not her flaming house! And when she's not obsessing about paint charts, she's hogging the computer or drinking my wine cellar dry." Dad takes one hand off the steering wheel and rakes it through his short dark hair, making it stand on end like a pineapple stalk.

"I thought Pauline was staying for just a couple of months," I say. "Doesn't she have a house in Portugal?"

"She's talking about selling that place and moving back here permanently. I've tried talking to Shelly about it, but she won't listen. She says if her mum doesn't want to go back to Portugal, then we can't make her. She also says that I'm useless with Gracie and that she wouldn't be able to cope without her mum around."

He sighs deeply. "I'm not naturally good with babies; they scare me a bit, to be honest. All that crying. And I am trying my best with Gracie. But Pauline isn't exactly making things easy at home. There's an atmosphere as soon as I walk in the door after work. I know what she secretly thinks of me. And she wonders why I stay late at work some nights. Ha! I can't bear to be anywhere near the stupid woman. You try living under the same roof as your mother-in-law, Amy."

"Dad, I'm thirteen! I'm hardly getting married anytime soon."

"Sorry, sorry, you're right."

Dad seems really down, so I try to say something positive. "At least Pauline helps with Gracie."

"That's just it. She doesn't, not anymore. I can't figure out why Shelly still wants her mum around. And we can't exactly talk about it with Pauline sitting in the next room. OK, I admit Pauline was great at the start, helping with night feeds and everything, but now she seems bored with all of that. She spends most of her time surfing the Internet and reading interior-decorating magazines." He sighs again. "I don't know what to do, Amy. I love Shelly, but I'm hopeless at all this family stuff."

That's an understatement—he abandoned me and Mum to set up home with Shelly, for goodness' sake. Poor Gracie! She deserves a good dad. I'm old enough to cope, but she's only tiny. He's not thinking of running out on her too, is he? I'm too depressed with this new thought to say anything back to him. I just stare out the window and watch the snake of cars ahead of us, all winding their way toward Dublin's shopping mecca.

As I walk toward the shopping center, my mood's so low it's practically in my Converses. Dad was eager to get to his golf game and didn't notice the way I snapped, "You'd better not be late collecting me," when I was getting out of the car.

Even though there are crowds of people milling around, I feel incredibly lonely. I think back to when Mum and Dad first separated. I was nine and they told me about it at Dublin Zoo, of all places. I remember feeling lost and deeply sad for weeks.

Mum got very depressed too. She used to spend all day in her dressing gown, drifting around the house like a zombie. She eventually snapped out of it, but it was horrible to live through. I felt so powerless. Dad had made his decision: he wanted to move on, start again with someone else, and there was nothing either Mum or I could do about it. And now it seems to be happening all over again to Shelly and Gracie. I once overheard Clover saying to Mum, "When the going gets tough, Art Green gets going. That's just how he is, Sylvie. Selfish to the core."

At least Mum's got Dave now. He's kind and caring and looks after her. He organized a romantic marriage proposal on a beach last year, which is something Dad would never think of, and they're getting married soon.

I love Dad, but sometimes I feel like punching him. Does he have any idea how lousy it is to have a part-time father? A dad who's never there when you get home from school, who forgets to turn up at sports games, who never appears at parent-teacher meetings, who has no idea what his daughter is reading, listening to, thinking, *feeling*, on a day-to-day basis? I really don't want that for Gracie. And I'm starting to feel a little sorry for Shelly too. Maybe I've been a bit hard on her. It sounds like Pauline isn't being all that helpful anymore, and I bet Dad's never once changed Gracie's nappy or given her a bath! And if he leaves, Shelly will have to bring up Gracie on her own. That's so sad that I don't even want to think about it.

I sit on the edge of the ornamental pool in the plaza, feeling cross and upset, and watch water from the fountain shoot up in jets. How dare Dad dump me here on my own and sneak off to play golf? Later, I bet he'll lie to Shelly and Pauline and tell them we spent a lovely afternoon together, strolling around the shops, holding hands, and swinging our arms, just like in a Disney movie.

My iPhone rings and I whip it out of my pocket.

"Yes?" I snap without checking who it is first. "What is it?"

"Whoa there, Beanie. Jeez Louise, jump out of bed on the wrong side this morning or what?" It's Clover.

"Sorry, it's just Dad. I'm so angry with him."

"What's he done now?" Clover doesn't sound surprised.

"I think he's about to do another runner. On Shelly and Gracie this time. He keeps arguing with Shelly about Pauline, apparently, and he said he wasn't cut out for family life."

Clover gives a long whistle. "Art Green, you never fail to disappoint me. The old 'not cut out for family life' chestnut." She says a very rude word under her breath. "Sorry, Beans, but your fatheaded father has to be the most selfish, self-absorbed eejit on the entire planet. And I can't believe he off-loaded his private woes on you. It's so inappropriate."

"I did tell him that. But Clover, what about Gracie? She's only three months old. It's so unfair."

"I agree, it's appalling. Look, I'm sure your poor-me pater's just mouthing off again. Even he isn't going to abandon a tiny baby like that. I just don't understand. He seemed so happy at the christening, so proud to be a dad again."

"Pauline's gotten worse, he says. He hates living in the same house as her."

Clover sighs. "Being in the same room as that woman gives me the heebie-jeebies. I can't imagine what it must be like to live with her. OK, I admit it does make me feel a teeny-weeny bit sorry for him. And why she'd want to live in Ireland when she can work on her leathery tan in Portugal I just don't know. . . . Beanie, where are you? I can hear splashing water. You're not about to throw yourself off a cliff or anything, are you?"

I give a short laugh. "Course not. I'm outside Dundrum Shopping Centre. Dad dumped me here. He's playing golf. I'm his beard."

"Beard?"

"You know, his cover. He told Shelly he was taking me shopping."

"Not helping my Hades-low opinion of him, Beanie. I have to work today, or else I'd come and hang out with you. That's why I'm ringing you, in fact. Guess who I'm interviewing tomorrow morning before her flight back to Budapest?"

"Claire Starr?"

"Bull's-eye, Bean Machine. The *Goss* was offered a last-minute spot, and Saffy asked me to cover it."

"Can I come too? And Mills?"

"Sorry, no can do, babes. Claire's unlikely to open up and dish her dirt if her own sister's listening in. Saffy said, and I quote, 'Find out if she is that Hungarian

Romeo's girlfriend or do not darken the doors of the *Goss* again, Clover.'" Saffy is Clover's editor at the *Goss* magazine, and she sounds pretty scary.

"Péter," I say. "Romeo's name is Péter. And Mills thinks they're together, but I'm not so sure. Watch the *Late Late Show* clip on the Internet and see what you think. Claire seemed a little stressed during the interview, especially toward the end. She seems to have something on her mind. She might like to talk to you about it. Off the record, I mean."

"Coola boola. Thanks, Beanie Baby. Nothing like a bit of insider info. I'll defo check out that clip. And if there is something bothering her, as you suspect, and she'd like to talk, then I'd be happy to listen. You are sweet, Beanie, always looking out for people. Look, must dash, research to run, dancers to dally with, you know how it is, but I'll catch you later, OK? And chin up. Art is just sounding off. I'm sure he doesn't mean it. He's crazy-golf about Gracie, you know that. And underneath it all, he does love you, hon, remember that. And I love you, babes, muchos much. Kiss, kiss." And with that she's gone.

I hope Clover's right that Dad was just sounding off. Clover's such a good listener. Maybe Claire will open up to her. They knew each other in school, so that might help. Talking about Claire has reminded me that I still haven't deleted her diary from my memory stick. I feel a dart of guilt. I'll do it as soon as I get home. I'll try to forget about it now and ring Mills. Maybe she can cheer me up or even join me at Dundrum. Besides, I'm dying to tell her the *Goss* goss.

Mills answers immediately, but she sounds a little disappointed to hear my voice. "Oh, hi, Amy. Sorry, I was hoping you were Bailey."

*Charming!* I try not to sound miffed as I say, "No, only me. Guess who Clover's interviewing tomorrow?"

"Claire, I know. Claire told me earlier. I think she's a bit nervous about talking to Clover, to be honest."

"Afraid of what my darling aunt might squeeze out of her?"

Mills giggles. "Exactly! Oh, there's another call coming through. It's Bailey. I'll ring you back, Ames, OK?" And the phone goes dead.

So I sit on the edge of the pool, waiting. Ten minutes pass, then fifteen, and I'm starting to get fed up, not to mention cold. I try Mills's phone again, but it goes straight to messages. A few minutes later I try once more, and finally she answers. "Sorry, Ames, I got distracted. Bailey's so funny sometimes and—"

I cut her off. "Look, Mills, I'm at Dundrum

Shopping Centre. Dad's abandoned me here while he goes off to play golf. Can you get the bus and join me? Seth's working with his mum this weekend, and I'm so lonely I could die. Woe is me." I'm only half joking. I really am feeling rather Billy-no-mates right now.

There's a long pause. "I'm really sorry, Amy, but I'm going to the cinema in Dun Laoghaire with Bailey. They're showing a Red Hot Chili Dogs concert, and he's mad keen to go."

"Chili *Peppers*," I correct. "And you don't even like them, Mills. Please? Who's more important, your bestest, bestest friend in the whole wide world, or your boyf? You can go to the cinema later."

"I have tryouts later."

"Tryouts?"

There's an awkward silence, but eventually she says, "I wasn't going to tell you unless I got on the squad, but the All Saints are looking for new members, and I thought I might give it a go. It looks fun, and you must admit, their uniforms are supercute."

The All Saints are the cheerleaders for our school's rugby team. We've always thought they were lamer than lame, but clearly that was, in fact, just me, not *we*. And their outfits are cute only if you think blue-and-white skater skirts that fan out when you move to show matching knickers with "All Saints" written across the bum in furry blue letters are cute. Which they most certainly are not!

"You're not serious? Mills, come on, you're hardly cheerleader material. And I mean that as a compliment. You know the All Saints have a secret tub under the changing rooms full of fake tan, and they make you swim through it every day, right? Then they throw you in an old dentist's chair, strap you down, and give you a lobotomy with a hockey stick."

"Amy, that's unfair. You don't have to be orange, or thick, for that matter. Nora-May Yang's on the squad, and she's really smart and cool. Don't be like this." (Nora-May's American and she started at Saint John's only a few weeks ago. She had to move from Boston to Dublin because of her mum's job. And Mills is right, she is nice.)

"Like what?"

"All snarky and mean. I'm really nervous about the tryouts. Can't you just wish me luck. Please?"

"Oh *merde*, then," I say.

"Amy!"

I give a laugh. "It's what all the ballet dancers say to each other before going onstage. It's like saying 'Break a leg.' So, *merde*." I put on my best D4 quasi-American accent. "But, like, be careful, babes.

Cheerleading is, like, prime D4 territory. Stay away from, like, Annabelle Hamilton and her, like, cronies. They are, like, so not to be trusted. Like, stick with Nora-May, OK?"

"I will. And I really am sorry I can't join you today, Ames. Honest."

After she hangs up, I try Seth on the off chance that he's around, even though I know he's helping Polly this weekend.

"Hey, Amy," he says, sounding pleased to hear from me, unlike Mills.

"You busy?" I ask.

"Just helping Polly get her stuff together for the birthday party later, and then we're going to catch some sort of photo exhibition in town. Everything OK?"

"Not really. Dad's dumped me in Dundrum while he's off playing golf."

He pauses for a beat. "I can blow off Polly if you like and come and meet you."

"No, don't do that. She'd be disappointed. But thanks for offering."

"What about Mills? I'm sure she'd be up for some Dundrum action. It's her second home."

"She's meeting Bailey and then she's trying out for the All Saints."

"That figures. I forgot to tell you about Bailey. The rugby coach spotted Boy Wonder playing British bulldogs during lunch last week and was so impressed that he asked him to join the team."

"Are we talking about the same Bailey Otis? The Bailey Otis whose fringe is so long he wouldn't be able to see a rugby ball, let alone run with one?"

"Sadly, I speak the truth. Turns out Bailey's a bit of a rugby head. Never misses a game on Sky Sports. It's his guilty secret. He's pretty good at playing it too, fast and slippery, ideal for the wing, apparently. Who would have thought, eh? Skinny bloke like him." He sighs. "Our boy has been tackled by the dark side."

"Don't go getting any ideas," I say.

"No intention of it, believe me. I'm no fan of cuts and bruises, or any sort of physical exertion, for that matter." He lowers his voice. "Although I can think of one notable exception, Amy Green. Working out the old lip muscles."

"Seth!"

He just laughs. "Look, Bailey's not going to change just 'cause he'll have his face mashed into the mud on a regular basis. He'll still be Bailey. And Mills will still be Mills, even in a cheerleader's outfit." I hear a voice in the background. "Polly's nagging me, better motor. She says hi, by the way."

"Tell her I say hi back, and I'll see you on Monday." At that moment I miss him so much it hurts. I kiss the phone softly.

"What was that?" he asks. "Did you just smooch your phone?"

"Absolutely not. 'Cause that would be too sad for words."

He laughs again. "See ya, Amy."

"Bye, Seth." I click off my mobile and stare down at it. Looks like I'm stuck here, alonio, then. I could ring Mum and ask her to come and collect me, but I don't want to get Dad into trouble. Yes, I'm livid with him, but getting Mum involved isn't the answer. No, I'll have to just ride it out. Dad said he'd collect me at one, so there's only another hour and a half to go.

It's cold out here, and even though I'm not in the mood for shopping, I can't stay outside all morning, so I pick my way through the crowds toward the main entrance to the shopping center. As I walk past Music City, I think back to the last time I was here, with Mills, Seth, and Bailey, on a double date. For Mills it was all about Bailey that day too.

I love Mills, but sometimes she drives me crazy. I know Bailey's important to her, but she's made me feel second best so many times recently, and it's starting to sting. Her decision to try out for the All Saints makes perfect sense after what Seth told me about Bailey joining the rugby team. She's never shown any interest in cheerleading before. She's clearly joining only because of him.

Lost in thought, I suddenly find myself in the Dundrum food hall. Feeling a desperate need to vent further, I plonk myself down at an empty table in the corner, pull my diary out of my bag, and start to write. My pent-up anger, hurt, and frustration flow onto the page like a dirty black oil slick. I'd forgotten how satisfying purging on paper can be.

**Saturday, December 1**

Dear Diary,

*Pógarooney,* I'm totally and utterly FED UP! I've been dumped for a game of golf and a dose of the Red Hot Chili "Dogs" by my idiot father and my boy-obsessed so-called BF and soon-to-be cheerleader. And let's face it, she'll be brilliant and they're bound to snap her up — Miss Amelia Not-So-Starry Starr . . .

♥ Chapter 4

"Where are the shopping bags, Amy?" Dad asks as soon as he spots me loitering outside the cinema, where we arranged to meet. He's twenty minutes late, and I was starting to worry that he'd forgotten all about me. He looks smiley and his eyes are bright. He must have won his round of golf.

I shrug. "Didn't see anything I liked. Besides, I'm broke."

He tut-tuts. "Sorry, how stupid of me. I should have given you some spending money. Why don't I buy you something now? We're a bit tight on time, so what about that shop over there?" He points across the plaza, and before I get the chance to say anything, he's striding toward the door, not even waiting to check if I'm following him. Next thing I know, we're at the bottom of an escalator, surrounded by beautiful clothes, and he's looking around, a slightly confused expression on his face. "I think I've been here before," he says. "With Shelly."

"That would be right," I murmur. "Dad, this is one of the most expensive shops in Ireland. It's called Harvey Nichols. It sells only designer stuff. We should probably try Penny's."

"No, we're here now. Anyway, if I want to treat my princess, I will."

I roll my eyes. "Dad, I'm thirteen. You really can't call me princess anymore."

Twenty minutes later, we're walking toward the car. This time I am swinging a shopping bag, a swish Harvey Nicks shopping bag, to be precise. Inside is a fab black-and-white-striped Sonia Rykiel T-shirt with glittery red cherries appliquéd over the right-hand shoulder. Clover will be so jealous. She loves Sonia with a passion. I'll have to keep a pretty sharp eye on my new tee or it will vamoose into her Bermuda Triangle of a wardrobe.

OK, so I know the top is a bribe, designed to keep my mouth zipped about the sneaky golf session, but I'm not above taking a bribe, especially when it's as fabarooney as this one.

Driving home on the M50 toward Castleknock, Dad is uncharacteristically quiet. After a few minutes, he turns down his Rolling Stones CD and says, "Amy?" with a serious voice. "That stuff I said to you earlier, about Shelly and Pauline? Don't say anything to your mum or Clover about it, OK? Especially not your mum. You're right. I shouldn't have brought it up. It wasn't appropriate." He's clearly afraid of getting an earful from Mum, and I don't blame him. When it comes to Dad, she's not exactly one for holding back.

Before I know what I'm saying, I blurt out, "You're not going to walk out on Shelly and Gracie, Dad, are you?"

He looks appalled. "No, no, of course not. What gave you that idea? It was all getting to me earlier, but I feel much better now. The golf really helped. I'll have to try to squeeze in a few more rounds soon. I was just mouthing off, Amy. I should have kept it to myself. I'm sorry. I didn't mean to worry you."

"That's OK," I say, feeling relieved. I'm still annoyed with him, but my mood has mellowed a little. Sharing my angst with my diary has really helped.

That evening, Dad insists I have dinner with him, Shelly, and Pauline before he drops me home. There's a lot of tension in the room. Dad and Pauline are barely speaking, and Shelly is picking at her food, looking tired and unhappy. She's wearing a navy Juicy tracksuit with milk stains on the shoulder, which isn't like her at all. Usually she's Gucci-ed up to the max, even at home.

I used to stay over a lot, pre-Gracie, but now Pauline's staying in my room, and to be honest, sharing a house with not one but two Lames isn't my idea of fun, so I haven't suggested it recently, even though I'd love to spend more time with Dad and Gracie.

"I spotted the Harvey Nichols bag in the hall, Amy," Pauline says, her lips pursed. "Bit expensive for a teenager, don't you think?"

"It wasn't my idea," I say. "It was Dad's."

"Art, you do spoil her. I hope you appreciate it, young lady," Pauline says with a sniff. "In my day, young people made do with hand-me-downs. None of this designer nonsense. Teenagers today are dreadfully privileged. No wonder the country's going to the dogs. The future of this great nation is in your hands, Amy. It's a serious responsibility."

"It is," I say mock gravely. "You're so right."

She throws me a daggers look, but I try to appear all innocent. She isn't fooled. "Art, you need to have words with your daughter," she says. "She's getting fierce cheeky. You clearly haven't taught her properly to respect her elders."

Dad's eyes darken, but before he gets a chance to open his mouth, Shelly says quickly, "Would you like some more wine, Mum?" and fills Pauline's empty glass to the brim again.

Shelly tops up her mum's glass so many times during dinner that afterward Pauline is California-surfer mellow.

"I do like a nice glass of fruity red wine," Pauline says. She gives a satisfied sigh and settles back in her chair. "It's like being back in Portugal. I always had a little tipple with my Dean after our siesta. Dean really knows his wine —"

There's loud squawking from the baby monitor, but Pauline ignores it. Shelly looks at Dad, but he doesn't appear to be moving either. "Don't worry, I'll get it," she says, pushing her chair back and getting to her feet. "I always do."

"Dad! Go and help her," I tell him as Shelly leaves the room. Pauline is still blabbering on about a man called Dean and doesn't seem to have noticed how upset Shelly looked when she left the room.

"Go on," I insist.

"Oh, what? Yeah, OK, good idea. Right," Dad says, as if it hadn't occurred to him. He really is hopeless. No wonder Shelly nags him. It's only after he's gone that I realize I am now stuck with the dreaded Pauline, alone.

"Where was I?" she asks me.

"In Portugal, having a siesta with someone called Dean."

She gasps, her cheeks turning lobster-pink, even under the heavy makeup. "Amy Green! That's a terrible thing to say. Dean's a perfect gentleman. He takes his siesta in his own villa, I'll have you know."

"Is Dean your boyfriend?" I ask, expecting her to tell me off again for being cheeky. But she doesn't.

"Not anymore," she says. The drink is clearly loosening her tongue. I can't believe she's telling me all this. "Stupid man and his stupid pub. He owns an Irish pub in Portugal, but he's from Birmingham, for goodness' sake. Birmingham, not Dublin!" She takes another loud slurp of her wine.

I shake my head. "Men. Nothing but trouble."

She looks at me a little crookedly. "And what would you know about it? Don't tell me you have a boyfriend, with that skin?"

The cheek of her! "Pauline, all teenagers have zits."

"Rubbish," she says. "My Shelly has always had the most perfect complexion, even during puberty."

"Bully for her," I mutter. "Anyway, for your information, yes, I do have a boyfriend, and strangely enough, he manages to overlook my skin and all my other glaring flaws. He's older than me too."

Pauline sighs. "Dean's also an older man. Sixty-eight! But you wouldn't know it, apart from the hair. He doesn't exactly have any." She slaps my hand, giving me a bit of a fright. "Anyway, do you know what my Dean does every single bloomin' day?"

I shake my head, hoping she isn't about to tell me some hideously inappropriate X-rated granny-on-grandpa tale.

"Plays golf." She shakes her head violently from side to side. Her hair must be practically varnished with spray, because not a strand moves. "Every single day. Golf, golf, golf." She hits my arm every time she says "golf." I pull it away before she bruises it. She packs quite a slap. No wonder she hates Dad playing. She clearly has a hang-up about it.

"I want to show you something." She staggers up from the table and fetches Dad's laptop from the kitchen counter. She plonks it down on the table and sits beside me. As I watch, she logs in to her Facebook account, taking three long, agonizing tries to get both the password—"sunnydays"—and her e-mail address right.

"There." She points at the screen. I look at the photo of a tanned bald man playing golf. She clicks on another picture, the same man, again playing golf. She bangs the screen closed, making me jump. I hope Dad's computer is all right.

"See, he's obsessed," she says. "I was so sick of it. So I told him, 'Dean,' I said, 'it's not acceptable to leave me to my own devices every single day. Aren't you afraid I'll run off with someone who pays me more attention? Someone who'll make an honest woman of me? For pity's sake, let's stop behaving like teenagers and get married. We've been together for a year now. It's the logical thing to do.' He's got the best-looking girlfriend in Portugal, but, no, he still won't marry me. Says things are just fine the way they are.

"When I came to Dublin to help my Shelly with little Grace, he didn't seem all that bothered that I'd be away for a couple of weeks. So I stayed for a few more weeks, and then a few more. I hoped it might bring him to his senses, you see—that he might miss me. But I don't think he does. Miss me, I mean. I think he's forgotten all about me."

Her face crumples (as much as it can with all the

Botox), and she gives an almighty howl and then starts to sob into her hands.

It's quite a scary sight. I grab some paper towel and hand it to her.

She dabs at her eyes, the paper towel turning black from her mascara. "Thank you, Amy. I don't know what came over me. And you mustn't tell a soul what I've just told you. Promise? I wouldn't want my Shelly finding out about any of this. She might get the idea that I'm not here to help with little Grace, which of course I am. I do love my little Gracie-Wacie. And Shelly was very close to her dad. She was devastated when he died, which is why I haven't told her about Dean yet. Looks like I won't need to now." She gives a little hiccup.

"Why don't you have a little nap on the sofa?" I suggest. "I'll tell Dad and Shelly not to disturb you."

She hiccups again. "What a good idea. Pity you're not as pretty as my Shelly. But I'm sure you'll find someone to marry you — eventually." With that, she staggers out of the kitchen.

I blow out my breath. Everyone in this family, including the in-laws and the out-laws, is completely crazy.

# ♥ Chapter 5

On Sunday afternoon, Clover bounds into my bedroom like a Labrador puppy and flops down on my bed.

"So, like, what's up, girlfriend?" she says in her best D4 voice. "Gimme a *C*. *C!* Gimme an *L*. *L!* Gimme an *O*. *O!*"

I laugh. "What are you doing, Clover?"

"OMG! Sylvie's just told me that Mills tried out for the All Saints. How could you let it happen, Greenster? Have I taught you *nada*? Cheerleading is so antifeminist that it's in another ballpark on another galaxy." She shakes her head and gives a deep, drawn-out sigh. In a French accent, she says, "Oh, ze young women of today, what is to become of zem? Tell me zat. *Moi*, Simone de Beauvoir, I am turning in my grave." Her accent changes to BBC News English: "And was it for this that poor old Emily Wilding Davison, RIP, threw herself under a horse? Answer me that." Clover's been taking a feminist literature course at Trinity College, and Simone de Beauvoir is one of her new heroes, along with Emmeline Pankhurst and other suffragettes who chained themselves to railings to get the vote for women. She smiles at me so I know she's only joking.

"I did try to talk her out of it," I say. "But it was hopeless. Her heart's set on wearing one of those tiny blue-and-white skater skirts."

"They are kinda cute," Clover admits.

"Clover! That's what Mills said. They are not!"

"But still, it's a sad state of affairs when your best friend takes up with the pom-pom poodles."

"Tell me about it."

"Maybe it's her way of stealing a bit of Claire's limelight," Clover says thoughtfully. "Can't be easy having a superstar sister. Maybe Mills is feeling a bit left out and wants to strut her own dance moves." Clover wiggles her chest backward and forward, making me giggle.

"Cheerleading is hardly ballet, Clover. And it's not about Claire, it's about Bailey. He's just joined the rugby team, and Mills wants them to be the Perfect Couple."

"It's still all a performance. Speaking of which, Claire Starr is one tough cookie."

"Of course, the interview. How did it go?"

"Nail-file rough at first. She seemed very wary of me. The PR woman sat in for most of it, but she had to leave toward the end to take a call, and Claire started to loosen up a bit after that. Unfortunately, I can't publish much from that part of the interview, as I promised Claire. She was in tears by the end of it. I think I might have asked her one question too many. I certainly didn't mean to upset her." Clover bites her lip.

"I'm sure it wasn't you, Clover. She's terrified about dancing her first big solo part."

"It's more than that, Beanie. You were right. Something is seriously upsetting Claire. I just don't know what. She was even talking about leaving the company and giving up ballet for good."

I gasp. "She can't! She loves dancing. It's all she's ever wanted to do."

"I know, and I wish we could fix things for her, but she wouldn't tell me what was wrong. Have you got any idea how we can find out, Beanie? Has Mills said anything?"

I can feel my face heating up because, yes, I do have an idea, but I can't possibly tell Clover about having Claire's diary. I'm too ashamed. I should never have made a copy of it in the first place, let alone read it.

"You OK, Beanie?"

"Yes, sorry, just thinking. . . . Writing the best interview ever and making Claire sound ultra-amazing might help. At least it would give her a confidence boost."

Clover grins at me. "It certainly can't do any harm. Glad you haven't lost your people smarts, babes. Now, my perfectly crafted piece has to be on Saffy's desk by first thing tomorrow morning. Wish me luck."

"*Merde*, Clover."

She gives a laugh. "Claire told me about that one. *Merde*, I like it. Better limber up." She knits her fingers together, twists her wrists out, and stretches her arms away from her chest. Then she rolls her shoulders, making an alarming bone-on-bone *click*. "Ah, that's better. Have to be writing fit to tackle this one, Bean Machine. I have a long night ahead of me. And let's hope Claire gets some of that old dancing diva-ness back before she has to charm her Romeo. Love you, babes. Kiss, kiss." She kisses the tips of her fingers and blows them at me. "'Good night, sweet prince, And flights of angels sing thee to thy rest!' Oops, I think that's *Hamlet*, not *Romeo and Juliet*. Note to self:

must brush up on my Shakespeare." And with that, she's gone.

I'm sitting on my bed, feeling down. Poor Claire. A bruised body will heal, but a bruised heart? Dancing is Claire's one great passion in life. If she has to give it up, she might never heal. I have to do something. I have to help her. I know it's wrong, but I *have* to read her diary! I'll start with Claire's very first entry.

Dear Diary,

Ta-da! I'm finally in Budapest. It's a bit of a dump, but I kind of like the rough edges. Makes it more interesting.

I've been here a week now and I've finally grabbed a few minutes to write up what's been happening. So — in a nutshell — I arrived last Saturday at Ferenc Liszt airport in Budapest and got a taxi to the academy.

Arriving at the academy was an eye-opener. I'm not sure what I was expecting, but, boy, is this place old, and, boy, are the rooms basic.

The building itself must have been spectacular in, oh, 1800, or whenever it was built, but I don't think it's been fixed up since. The whole place smells old and musty, of ancient crumbling plaster, bleach, and damp washing. More on the washing in a mo'!

When you walk through the big wooden door, there's this humongous entrance hall, with a smooth stone floor and a huge marble staircase marching up the back wall.

So there I was on Saturday morning, exhausted after getting up at four a.m. to catch the mad-early flight, struggling through the door with all my luggage, and inside there were masses of girls and guys milling around the hallway with bags. Theirs were much smaller than my whoppers, of course — you'd swear I was going to Outer Mongolia. Mum and Dad even made me bring toilet paper, just in case.

Anyway, the others all seemed to know one another. They were chatting in groups of three or four. I was feeling a bit lost and out of place until a blond girl started talking to me.

"You're the Irish girl everyone's been talking about, yes?" she said. "Lucky for you, I like Ireland. U2, yes? Bono rocks for an old man. OK, Irish, you and I will share a room, yes? Stay there and mind my bag." Before I could answer, she'd dumped a long black-canvas bag at my feet and run over to talk to a tiny old woman with white hair in a bun and small dark eyes like a bird's.

Then the girl shoved her way back through the crowd that was now clamoring noisily around the woman and sprinted up the stairs. She was followed several seconds later by a stream of boys and girls, all elbowing one another and shouting. I hadn't a clue what was happening, so I just stood in the hallway, minding her bag and hoping she'd come back.

And she did — half an hour later.

After grabbing her bag, she told me to follow her. When I asked where to, she said, "To our room, of course. The best room in the whole academy. If someone realizes I've gone, they'll steal it. Move!"

So now I have a Slovakian roomie — Lana — and the best room in the academy. It's a tiny space with two squeaky metal beds and no outside window. The only light comes through the glass door, which opens onto a long conservatory. At first, it seemed an odd place to pick — it's just beside the washroom and we have to walk through all the damp leotards and tights drying on racks to get to our door — but Lana says it's the warmest room in the whole place. The windows of the other rooms freeze up in winter. And as long as you don't mind getting slapped in the face by wet tights now and then, it's heaven.

Washing is a BIG DEAL in the academy. We all have to do our own by hand, and there's no tumble dryer, so everything takes ages to dry. Honestly, it's like living on the set of *Annie* or something. I asked Lana if there was a launderette nearby, but she just laughed and said, "You think you will have time to waste outside class? Ha! Get used to it, Irish."

Lana showed me around the academy on our first full day and also made me do some exercises in one of the ballet classrooms. There are six in total: three on this floor and three more on the first floor. Each one has large windows, an upright piano, and a stool or bench for the teacher to sit on, and, of course, huge floor-to-ceiling mirrors.

"This will be our classroom," Lana said, waving her hand around one of the classrooms on the first floor. "It is a big honor to be in Madame Irina's class. I hope you do not mess it up, Irish."

Madame Irina János is the principal and artistic director of the academy. She used to be a prima ballerina here and is almost as famous in Hungary as Olga Varga.

Lana told me to begin the exercises with some ten-dus, so after some warm-up pliés at the barre, I started doing them, stretching my leg out and brushing my toes over the worn wooden floorboards.

Lana stood watching me, her hands on her hips. When I had finished, she said my tendus were poor. I was shocked. No one has ever called them poor before. I've always been the best in the class at everything. But Lana told me to do them again, faster.

I tried once more, and she still shook her head. "But Irina must have seen something in you, Irish," she said.

I wasn't taking it. I've worked hard to get here, and I'm not going to let anyone discourage me. I asked her to show me how they should be done.

Standing in front of me at the barre, she whipped her foot out and in again like lightning. I couldn't believe it—her movements were so sharp, so strong. And she was right, my tendus were poor in comparison. I was determined to make them better.

I tried again and again. Each time she said, "Faster. More power." Finally, I was just too exhausted to do any more. She shook her head. "They're going to eat you up here, Irish, and spit you out."

"I don't taste very nice," I said, and then I steeled myself. I flicked my foot out and in again, as hard and as fast as I could.

Lana looked only mildly impressed. I was determined to get my tendus perfect by the following morning's class, so I asked Lana how long we could stay in the classroom. She smiled and said, "As long as you like, Irish. There may be hope for you yet."

Later, Lana gave me another piece of advice. She told me never to smile, talk back, or cry in class. Ever. I told her I understood, even though it all sounded weird. Miss Smitten had warned me about Hungarian dance classes and how tough they were, but come on, what teacher would make you cry? Besides, I never cry, it's just not me. (I hadn't been in one of Madame Irina's classes at that stage — and boy was that another eye-opener!)

Oops, better stop. I can hear Lana slapping her way back through the wet tights. I'll write soon, Diary, promise. And I'll tell you all about my very first class with the Miss Terrifying herself, Madame Irina!

*Szia!* That means "See you soon" in Hungarian. I'm picking up a little bit every day, but don't talk to me about the Hungarian language classes — yuck!

Claire Starr, future prima ballerina xxxxx

I stop reading and sit back in my chair, still lost in Claire's world of damp tights and tendus. I'd forgotten how strong and self-assured Claire used to be, certain that she could be one of the best dancers in the world and determined to get to the top. From what Clover said, unless Claire can tap into that old confident self again, her whole ballet career could be at stake. And so far, Claire's diary hasn't given me any clues as to what's troubling her or how we might be able to help her.

# ♥ Chapter 6

Claire's diary reminds me to write in my own, and I have to get something off my chest.

Sunday, December 2

Dear Diary,
Ten Reasons Why Mills Starr Drives Me Crazy!

Number 1:
I hate the fact that Mills always chooses Bailey over me. Take today, for example. Mills rang me this morning to say that she couldn't come over until this evening, as she was still tired after the tryouts yesterday. And then she let it slip

that Bailey was coming over. "I thought you were too tired to see anyone," I said.

After the call, I was fuming. I know Bailey's great and everything, and yes, OK, übercute, but the way Mills goes on about him, you'd think he was some sort of reincarnated Greek god. Which he's not! He's a normal mortal. He belches and farts just as much as the next guy. Mills is just too blind to see it.

Number 2:
I hate the way she's always flicking her hair around like a D4. I know she doesn't mean to do it, and she has fantastic hair — all glossy and perfect — but it's still annoying. And if she becomes a cheerleader, she's bound to hair-flick even more. It'll be like hanging around with My Little Pony.

Which brings me to Number 3:
The whole perfect thing. Why does she have to be so perfect all the time? Perfect hair. Perfect teeth. Perfect skin. Perfect neat, ironed uniform. Perfect grades. Perfect family . . . which all combine to make her the Perfect Cheerleading Girlfriend for the newly crowned Rugby God. All hail, Bailey Otis!

And this brings me to another gripe . . .

Number 4:

This whole All Saints thing. Mills hasn't stopped going on about the tryouts, telling me every little detail of her All Saints experience and how amazing Nora-May is at cheering and how in Boston, where Nora-May's from, cheerleading is recognized as a proper sport and how difficult some of the moves are to remember, yadda, yadda, yadda . . . Not one word about what happened in Dundrum, with Dad and everything. No "How are YOU, Amy? How was YOUR day yesterday, Amy? Sorry for abandoning you for the All Saints and my boyfriend, Amy." Nothing!

I'm convinced that, despite all her Nora-May talk, Mills is only taking up cheerleading so that she and Bailey can be the "Perfect Couple." It is further evidence of the Starr Perfection Curse. Which poor Claire also seems to suffer from, by the way.

My clearly deluded friend has been watching too many old American teen movies. You know the ones: where the Quarterback dates the Head Cheerleader. Doesn't Mills realize that the Quarterback and Cheerleader never end up together? The Quarterback always finds love with the Geek Girl, and the Cheerleader always runs off with the Bad Boy.

Mills may be in for a fall.

I sit back and think for a moment, but I can't come up with any more "reasons," so I cross out the number ten at the top and replace it with a four. Looking back over the list, I start to feel bad. Here I am, moaning on about Mills in my diary when Claire is finding it so hard to cope back in Budapest. I need to get my priorities in order. My life is pretty rosy compared to Claire's at the moment. So I add:

OK, now I've got all that off my chest, Diary, I feel a whole heap better. Mills may be annoying sometimes, but I love her anyway, and let's face it, I'm hardly perfect either. Despite everything, she is the best friend a girl could wish for, and that's a fact!

I drop my pen, sit back in my chair, and smile to myself, Mills's aggravating flaws almost forgotten. This diary thing really is great! Talk about cheap therapy!

♥ Chapter 7

Later that evening, I'm keeping an eye on Alex in the bath while Mum settles Evie to sleep (which can take a while) and wondering if Mills will visit, like she promised. I feel bad for ranting about her in my diary. It wasn't fair, and I didn't really mean it. I was just feeling ratty. I vow to rip out the page as soon as Mum relieves me from Alex duty. I can hear her singing to Evie, so she won't be long.

Evie's starting to talk now and can even say my name — sort of. She calls me "Mee-mee," copying Alex, who still calls me this, even though he can say Amy perfectly well now if he wants to. I don't mind. It's kind of cute. Alex is "Ahhhh-ex," but Clover's name is the funniest. She's "Oooo-vaaaa," to which

Clover adds, "and out," making herself laugh like a hyena. "Get it, Beanie? Over and out?" I just roll my eyes at her.

Alex is more troll than toddler, stomping around the house, destroying things. His train obsession is getting worse too. He will only wear Thomas the Tank Engine underpants now. (Mum's trying to potty-train him at the moment, and there are tiny "Thomas" underpants drying on every heater. Let's not go there!) But he is megacute, with a puffball of superblond hair, big gooey blue eyes and a funny round potbelly. At the moment, he's standing up in the bath, covered in bubbles from head to toe, giggling away to himself. He bends down and scoops up some water in his hand, clearly about to chuck it at me.

"Don't even think about it, Alex," I tell him, tipping the water out of his hand. "No! And sit down before you slip, OK?"

"O-K, Mee-mee."

The doorbell rings downstairs.

"Can you get it, Amy?" Mum calls from Evie's room. "I've nearly gotten her to sleep."

"No problem." I look at Alex sternly. "Stay here, buster, and no funny business, understand?"

He nods. "I good boy, Mee-mee."

I dash down the stairs and swing the door open. It's Mills, stepping from foot to foot and looking a little awkward.

"Hiya, Mills."

"Look, Amy, I'm sorry. I was going on and on about tryouts earlier, and I completely forgot to ask you about your dad's house and to say sorry for not coming to meet you in Dundrum yesterday."

"It's OK. I understand," I say, feeling even worse about my diary rant. "Dundrum wasn't so bad in the end. Dad got me a top at Harvey Nicks. Sonia Rykiel, no less."

Mills looks at me blankly.

"She's a French designer. It's the most expensive thing I've ever owned."

"Cool! Can I see it?"

"Sure, come on up. Alex is in the bath, and I'm supposed to be supervising him. Why don't you wait in my room while I pull him out? It won't take long. The top is hanging on the back of my door if you want to have a look."

Mills goes to my bedroom while I deal with Alex. I walk back into the bathroom and gasp. "*Pógarooney*, goblin boy, what have you done?"

He's lying tummy down on the floor tiles, completely naked, one hand on the back of his head.

"I shark," he says. "I eat you." He grabs my leg and chomps it with his surprisingly sharp baby teeth. Luckily, I'm wearing jeans or he might have broken the skin.

"Ow! Alex, stop that. And stand up. There's water all over the floor."

"Sea," he explains. "Shark like sea."

"What's wrong with being a shark in the bath?" I ask him, losing patience.

"Too small," he says. "I big shark."

"Right, Mr. Shark," I say, holding his arm firmly. "You're in for it. Mum!"

I wrap a large towel around Alex, sling him over my shoulder in a quasi-fireman's lift while he squeals with delight, and walk into the hall. I bump straight into Mills, who is running out of my room. There's a funny look on her face. Her lips are pressed together and her cheeks are bright pink.

"What's up, Mills?" I ask her.

Saying nothing, she just pushes past me and runs down the stairs.

"Mills, where are you going?" I call after her.

She swings around at the bottom of the stairs and clutches the banister. "Home!" Her eyes are welling up.

"Why? You've only just gotten here. What's wrong?"

"You hate me. You think I'm annoying and stupid." Her face crumples and tears start spilling down her cheeks. "*And* you were mean about my sister. I thought we were best friends. What kind of person are you, Amy Green?"

The whole world stops. The only thing I can hear is my own heart thumping wildly in my chest. Then I realize what Mills is talking about. I left my diary open on my desk, which means . . .

"Mills, don't go," I say frantically. "I can explain. I was in a bad mood. I didn't mean any of it —"

But it's too late. She's already out the front door and banging it behind her.

"What's all the commotion?" Mum asks, appearing in the hallway.

"I shark, Mummy," Alex says, gnashing his teeth in her direction. "I eat you."

"Was that you making all that noise, young man?" she asks him. "Here, let me take him, Amy. He's heavy."

"I'll clean up the bathroom," I say, relieved that Alex has managed to cover for me. My stomach is churning. How could I have been so stupid? What kind of eejit leaves her diary on show like that?

Mum smiles at me. "Thanks, pet. And who was at the door, by the way?"

"Just Mills popping in to ask about some homework due tomorrow."

Mum tilts her head. "Are you sure everything's all right? You're very pale."

"I'm just tired. Busy weekend." I turn away from her, hoping she hasn't spotted the tears starting to prick at my eyes because I have a horrible feeling that absolutely nothing is all right. I think I've just lost my best friend. And it's all my own stupid fault.

# ♥ Chapter 8

Later, to try to take my mind off things and to stop Mills's words from ringing in my ears — *What kind of person are you, Amy Green?* — I read another of Claire's diary entries. If I can't help myself, at least I can try to help someone else.

Dear Diary,
I'm back! Now . . . what was I writing about? Ah, yes, my very first class with Madame Irina.

Hang on, no, I should start by wishing you a very happy Saint Patrick's Day. Lana ordered some Cadbury's chocolate for me on the Internet and gave it to me this morning over breakfast.

"Happy Paddy's Day, Irish," she said, and then proceeded to eat most of the bar herself. I didn't mind, though. It was nice of her to remember. I wonder what Mills and Mum and Dad are doing today. They love Paddy's Day. They always go to the parade and cheer on all the floats. I miss Mills. I must remember to ring her this week.

Anyway, back to my debut class. We had a full lesson of tendus. I did my best, but even with Lana's coaching, I was way behind the other girls. But when Madame called me an unfit, flabby, lazy, rich girl, I remembered what Lana had said and didn't say a word. I just took it all on the chin and stayed completely silent. It seemed to be the right thing to do. Madame stopped criticizing me when I didn't flinch and moved on to pick holes in another girl's technique instead.

As for smiling in class, there isn't much to smile about, so I don't need to remember to keep a straight face. It's exhausting and soul destroying. Miss Smitten warned me that Hungarian teachers are not like Irish teachers. They believe in hard work and total 100 percent dedication to dance. I didn't think it would be *this* bad. But I do know that I'm learning so much every day and taking baby steps toward becoming the dancer of my dreams. I know all the hard work will pay off in the end.

I've worked out that Madame Irina's hardest on the

girls she thinks have the most potential. That seems to be me and Zsuzsanna, one of the Hungarian girls. She pushes us to our limits. I hate it when she prods me with her stick or criticizes me, but I know she's just trying to make me a better dancer, so I take it.

Today, Madame Irina moved me to the middle of the back barre, which is the best spot in the whole class. Nóra, one of the other Hungarian girls, had to give up her place and move to the side barre. If looks could kill, I'd be in a Hungarian morgue right now. But that's OK. I'm here to work, not to make friends. Besides, I have Lana, who may be direct but is also funny and kind underneath her tough exterior.

And wonder of wonders! Madame finally said my tendus were "OK for a rich girl."

I told her that my family was not rich, forgetting what Lana had said about not talking back. I couldn't help myself. I just wanted to set the record straight. I said I came from a normal Dublin family and that my dad worked in a post office. He's some sort of accountant for the postal service, so it's kind of true.

Madame just gave a loud *pah,* and said I'd probably been spoiled all my life. Then she grabbed my arm and pinched my skin between her bony fingers and said, "Fat, fat, fat. Lazy, lazy, lazy."

Now, OK, my arms aren't as toned as the other girls'

yet, but they soon will be. Lana has me doing special exercises to strengthen all my muscles. And with that and the food in the cafeteria — which is basically different versions of goulash and cabbage every day, plus hard, chewy bread and odd fried-doughy things that taste of grease and I refuse to eat — I won't be flabby for long.

I stuck out my chin and said I wasn't lazy and I deserved to be here. I've been practicing every night after class until I drop, both with Lana and on my own, and "lazy" wasn't fair.

Madame Irina's eyebrows lifted at that, but she seemed amused rather than angry. "We shall see, Irish girl," she said. Which was better than being called "rich girl," I guess.

I knew better than to say anything else. I half expected her to move me back to a side barre, but she didn't. As Lana said, maybe there's hope for me yet.

Speaking of practice, I'd better run. Lana's expecting me . . .

Until next time, Diary, *szia!*

Claire Starr, future prima ballerina xxxxx

# ♥ Chapter 9

I wait by the letter box on Monday morning for Mills, but she doesn't appear. She's clearly avoiding me. I'll have to travel to school on my own. Maybe I'll have to spend the whole day alone. School without Mills . . . The thought makes me shiver.

I take a deep breath, willing back the tears that are threatening to spill down my cheeks. I feel so on edge this morning, and the exhaustion isn't exactly helping. I couldn't get to sleep last night. My mind and emotions just wouldn't shut down. I'm so angry with myself for being such an idiot, and I feel cutting guilt at upsetting Mills. If only I'd kept to the facts in my diary, like Claire does in hers, and not gone off on a self-indulgent moan, everything would be all right now.

I rang and rang and rang Mills's mobile last night, but she wouldn't answer, and eventually she turned it off. So I tried the house line, but Sue said Mills wasn't feeling well and couldn't come to the phone. Then I stopped by, which was ultramortifying, as Sue answered the front door, her face all red and embarrassed.

"I'm sorry, Amy," she said. "Mills doesn't want to speak to you right now." She lowered her voice. "She won't tell me what's happened, but I'm sure she'll calm down in a few days. Just give her some time. This has happened before, remember, and you managed to patch things up. You two are such good friends, it would be an awful shame if, well, you know . . ." Sue gave me a kind, open smile just like Mills's, making me feel even worse. Why, oh, why had I written those ridiculous things in my diary? Mills is a brilliant friend and I don't deserve her. If only she'd just talk to me, let me explain . . .

In school, things are not looking good. Mills has been ignoring me all morning, turning away whenever I try to speak to her, and people are starting to notice. Annabelle Hamilton corners me at the lockers at first break. "You and Amelia having a tiffy wiffy, are you?" she asks. Nina is standing just behind her, peering at me like a vulture, all beady little eyes and scrawny neck.

"Leave me alone, Annabelle." I slam my locker shut harder than strictly necessary.

"Temper, temper," Nina scolds. She opens her mouth to say something else but is interrupted by Sophie. "Hey, girls," she calls out. "The results of the All Saints tryouts are up on the notice board. We're all still in. Natch! And a couple of the newbies got picked too."

Before Sophie gets a chance to say who, Annabelle and Nina are racing down the corridor. Normally I'd rather follow a farting frog than Annabelle Hamilton, but I do desperately want to talk to Mills, and I know she'll be keen to find out if she's made the cut, so I tag along, walking several feet behind the D4s and trying to ignore their gibes.

"What's that funky perfume Green's wearing, girls? Anyone recognize it?" Annabelle says, sniffing the air. "I'm getting Parfum Desperation — no, wait, it's Eau de Self-Loathing." They all cackle like witches.

Mills is standing at the notice board, staring up at a sheet of paper and biting her lip anxiously. Nora-May is beside her, beaming. She's obviously back on the squad. But it looks like Mills isn't.

"Sorry you didn't make it, Mills," I say.

Mills's eyes are still fixed on the notice board. "Thanks for your vote of confidence, Amy. Actually, I'm in."

"Congratulations," I say quickly, hoping she'll at least look at me. "You'll make a great cheerleader."

She looks at me now, her eyes steely. "Don't be so sarcastic, Amy. It doesn't suit you. And I have things to discuss with the other All Saints, so if you don't mind . . ." She tosses her head at me, her ponytail swishing behind her. "Vamoose!"

"Things to discuss? As if." Annabelle laughs nastily. "Let's get this straight, Amelia Bedelia. You may be, like, on the squad, but that does not mean we have to speak to you outside training. I bet you were picked just because Bailey Otis is your boyfriend. So if you're, like, looking for new fwendy-wendys, then you can forget it. Why don't you crawl back to your primordial pond with Green, 'cause that's where you both belong, with the lower species."

Mills's face goes bright pink, then white, and she looks completely humiliated.

"Mills, don't pay any attention—" I start to say, but she cuts me off.

"Just shut up, Amy," she says. "And leave me alone."

"Annabelle Hamilton, who died and made you

president?" Nora-May asks, hands on her hips. She's much taller than Annabelle and has wide, strong shoulders. She looks pretty imposing. "Now, scoot and leave us *proper* cheerleaders to talk."

Annabelle pokes the All Saints notice with a false nail. "What does it say here? Gosh, I seem to be head cheerleader. Fancy that. So, actually, I am in charge, Nora-May, and don't you forget it. You're just, like, a blow-in. Go back to China."

"Boston," Nora-May says without blinking. "And I'm not scared of you, Annabelle. I've been cheering for years and I'm way better than you are. And I'm going to make it my business to train Mills up too. Bring — it — on."

"You should be quaking in your cheap, tacky shoes, Nora-May," Annabelle says, her eyes narrowing. "You're, like, so messing with the wrong girl." And she flounces off, followed by Sophie and Nina.

"Bravo, Nora-May, you showed her," Mills says, ignoring me. "Tell me all about your cheering in Boston. I'm dying to hear about it."

I walk away as Mills chatters on happily to Nora-May. I feel as low as a slug. I've been replaced.

That evening Mum comes into my room. I've been lying in bed, snuggled under my duvet since coming home from school. I told her I wasn't feeling well, but I think she senses that something else is up.

"Mills dropped this off," she says, handing me a long white envelope sealed firmly shut. "She didn't want to come in. What's wrong, Amy? Have you two fallen out again?"

"No, of course not." I take the envelope from her and stare down at it, willing her to leave me alone so that I can look inside.

She gets the message. "I'll be downstairs if you need me. I know you don't feel up to eating, but I'll bring you up a tray with some soup and toast a little later, OK? You won't get better unless you eat. There are some nasty bugs doing the rounds at the moment and you do look a little flushed."

I try a smile, but I'm sure it's not very convincing. "Thanks, Mum."

As soon as she's gone, I rip open the envelope. It's a letter, written on a sheet of paper. I unfold it and instantly recognize the neat, perfect handwriting.

Amy,

I'm sorry for disappointing you. I'm sorry for being so perfect. I'm sorry for treating Bailey the way he deserves to be treated, with kindness and respect. I'm sorry for being such a ditz and for getting the Red Hot Chili Peppers' name wrong.

I wince. She must have read the entry I wrote while waiting for Dad at Dundrum Shopping Centre as well. Ouch!

But most of all, I'm sorry for wasting so much time worrying about you. At least I now know how you really feel about me. I had no idea you've been laughing at me behind my back all this time. How can you live with yourself, Amy Green? From now on, we are over, Amy, finished. Kaput. We are no longer friends.

Please don't try to fix this. Don't visit or ring me and beg for my forgiveness. Don't ask Clover to talk to me, and stop following me around in school. It won't work. It's too late. I don't want anything to do with you, get it? And leave Seth and Bailey out of this. I beg you, do one final thing for me — just leave me alone.

You are now officially dead to me. This is good-bye.

Your airhead ex-friend,
Mills Starr

♥ Chapter 10

Without Mills by my side, school is a total nightmare on Tuesday. I try to respect her wishes and leave her alone, but it's so hard. Our lockers are next-door neighbors, we have a lot of the same classes, and then there's Bailey and Seth to contend with — the boys are so close these days that you need a knife to separate them.

"Mills," I say in a low voice at break as she's fishing her Irish books out of her locker. "I know you don't want anything to do with me at the moment, but that will change, right? You'll forgive me, won't you? I know you need some time, but Seth was hoping to have us all over on Friday after school and —"

She bangs her locker door closed so hard that it sounds like a gun firing. Then, without even looking at me, she bundles her books into her bag and speeds off down the corridor.

"Mills," I say, running after her.

She spins around and glares at me. "I'm warning you, Amy, stop following me."

"Or what?"

She just shakes her head. "You're being pathetic. Go and find someone else to annoy." She gives a short laugh. "Oh, no, that's me, isn't it? The annoying one." Then she starts walking again, leaving me standing there, staring at her back.

I make my way slowly back up the corridor to find Seth leaning against my locker, waiting for me. "Hey, Amy," he says, smiling easily. "You all right? You look like someone's just murdered your hamster."

I sigh. I may as well tell him. He'll find out eventually anyway. "I had a run-in with Mills."

He doesn't seem surprised.

"You know, don't you?" I say. "About Mills reading my diary."

He nods. "Bailey said something about it, yeah. She's just a bit upset. She'll snap out of it. Give her time."

"I'd written loads of stuff about her, Seth, bad

stuff. I was in a mood, and I took it out on her. But I didn't even mean half of it. It was a horrible thing to do. I'm so ashamed. What was I thinking?"

He puts his finger on my lips. "Forget about it. At least she knows what an amazing kisser I am now."

"I don't write about you, Seth," I insist, willing my face not to go scarlet, because it's a complete lie. I documented our first kiss in forensic detail. "I've got far more important things to cover. Like world peace, and who's going to win *America's Next Top Model*."

"Good to see you smiling, kiddo," he says, pulling me into a hug. "Forget about Mills. I'll be your best friend instead."

"Thanks, Seth," I whisper. I'm so lucky to have him on my side.

I'm finding it impossible to concentrate on my homework. Instead, I'm sitting at my desk, twanging an old red rubber band that's looped over my fingers like it's a tiny guitar.

Mum sticks her head through the doorway. "How are you getting on, Amy? Need any help?"

Why do olds always ask this? It drives me crazy. It's not like she's going to do my homework for me. She's clearly just spying on me, making sure I'm not, oh, playing with a rubber band or something childish like that.

"Do you mean that?" I ask, calling her bluff. "About helping?"

"Yes," she says cautiously.

"OK, then, you can write my English essay for me. It's on death in the Shakespearean sonnets, and then you can research the Greek gods for this Parthenon project I have to do for classics."

She looks taken aback. "I can't *write* your essay for you, Amy. That wouldn't be right."

"But you can look up the Greek gods for me on the Internet," I suggest. "Please! I have so much work, and you did offer to help."

"I suppose. But I have to put Evie and Alex to bed first. And, um, clean up the kitchen, and deal with the washing, and —"

"Ha! Got you. It's fine, Mum, I'll manage all on my lonesome. But can I use the laptop up here for my research?"

She looks relieved. "Of course. And I'll check on you again later. No Facebooking now." She wags her finger at me, mock strict.

I smile to myself. There's nothing like a bit of emotional blackmail to get what you want. Normally I have to use the laptop downstairs, where Mum can keep an eye on me. She's convinced all teens waste their lives on Facebook. But, come on! How else are we supposed to have a social life when we're chained to our desks?

In fact, checking Facebook is the first thing I do once I've set the laptop up on my desk. Obviously! For a second, I don't notice anything wrong. Then it hits me. There are no posts from Mills. Usually there are loads — Mills is Facebook crazy. Her mum and dad let her have a page just a few months ago, and she's been obsessed ever since. I check my friends list, but I can't find her at all. She's defriended me. I can't believe it. It seems so brutal, so permanent.

I click out of Facebook and stare at the computer screen. There's no way I can focus on my homework now. But I still type "Greek gods" into Google and then click on allaboutgreekgods.com in case Mum comes in and catches me doing nothing and gives me an earful, making an already terrible day even worse.

"The Greeks did not believe in a single, all-powerful god," the website reads. "They had many gods and goddesses who controlled both nature and fate. But the chief of all the gods was Zeus, god of thunder and lightning."

Mum sticks her head around the door again and looks suspiciously at the screen.

Ha, foiled her!

"Fascinating stuff here about Zeus," I say.

She smiles at me. "I'm really proud of you, Amy. Knuckling down to do your homework like that. I'll be downstairs if you need me."

I stare vacantly at the Greek gods website for a few more minutes, but the words start to swim in front of my eyes and then Mills's face seems to materialize on the screen, like something out of *Doctor Who*. Why was I so stupid? I've lost the best friend ever, and I have only myself to blame.

# ♥ Chapter 11

"Hey, Beanie, good to see you. What's up?" Clover looks up from her desk and swivels around in her black-leather chair. It's Wednesday afternoon. I usually hang out with Mills on Wednesdays, but today I'm all alone, so I decided to visit Clover's "office," a customized shed at the back of Gramps's garden.

"Nothing much." I slump down on a small red sofa.

"Things with Mills any better?"

"No," I say gloomily. "She's still not talking to me. It's been three days now, and it's doing my head in. I feel so miserable, Clover. I've tried talking to Seth about it, but he says Mills will snap out of it eventually. Anyway, he has other worries. He's concerned about Bailey. The other guys on the rugby team want him to chug this creatine stuff to bulk up 'cause he's being pushed around on the pitch. It's a kind of diet supplement. Is it safe, Clover? Do you know anything about it?"

"It's funny you should say that, about creatine, I mean," Clover says. "I have a letter here from a girl asking a very similar question. Her brother plays for Monkstown College, in fact."

"Makes sense. There's a big match coming up, Monkstown against Saint John's. They're both favorites for the Junior Cup."

"Let me see if I can find it." Clover rummages in the top tray of her tower of plastic boxes. "Bingo!" She hands me the printout of a letter and I read it.

Dear Clover and Amy,

I have a serious problem, and I need your help. My twin brother, Happo (Harry), is only in the second year, but he's really good at rugby and he's already on the Junior Cup team. That is a big deal in Monkstown College because it's such a megarugby school, as I'm sure you know only too well!

Happo's started taking this weird powder called Xtra-Tone Creatine X5 every day to "get ripped" (you have to say this in a silly American accent, like he does). He spoons it into a sports bottle, mixes it with water, and then forces it down, even though he says it tastes disgusting. He doesn't want me to tell Mum 'cause she'll only "freak out."

I don't want to sound like a wuss, but I'm worried about him. You see, when he was born, he had this heart condition and nearly died. What if this creatine stuff damages his heart?

Happo says I'm being stupid, that all the lads take it. In fact, he suspects some of them are on steroids too, even though they're totally 100 percent banned and the rugby coach would have a fit if he found out about it. But the Monkstown lads are all so obsessed with the Cup, they'd do anything to win.

I'm megaworried here, girls, and I don't know what to do. If I say something to Mum, she'll probably stop Happo from playing rugby and he'd kill me. He's mad into it. All he wants to do with his life is be a pro player. I have to do something, though. What if this creatine stuff is really dangerous?

Please help!

Dominique, 14, in Dublin

I hand the letter back to Clover and give a whistle. "*Siúcra ducra*, that's serious stuff."

"No kidding, Beanie. And if guys in Monkstown and Saint John's are both using this creatine, it's bound to be widespread. I didn't know much about it, so I did some digging. It seems legit enough stuff. Apparently it increases strength and builds lean muscle mass, and it occurs naturally in the body." She puts on a science-bod voice: "According to our extensive research, no lab rats have died while using creatine. In fact, it seems to lengthen their life, if anything." She goes back to her normal voice. "Used properly, that is, and in the right doses. Funny, isn't it? Most girls want to lose weight, but dudes want to 'get ripped.' Sad, really. We're never happy with what we've got. No, what concerns me is that this creatine might act as a gateway to stronger stuff, like the steroids Dominique mentioned. I've read about steroids and they do have side effects, serious ones. And they *can* damage the heart."

"So, what do we tell Dominique? And Seth?"

"I don't know, Beans. Any brain waves yourself, the elf?"

"Well," I say, an idea burning. "Remember when we first went into the problem-solving business? You said we weren't just going to sit back and answer letters from the comfort of your office, we were going to jump straight in feetfirst and get our hands dirty. 'Up close and very, very personal,' I think were your words."

"Where are you going with this, Beanie?"

"Clover, I think I feel a plan coming on. We're going to e-mail Dominique right now and ask for her brother's training timetable. Maw-ha-ha-ha." I give my best evil-genius Disney laugh.

# ♥ Chapter 12

"Oi, Beanie!" Clover bellows. "Over here!" It's after school the next day. Clover's stopped in the middle of the Saint John's driveway and is hanging out of the window of her red Mini Cooper and waving like a lunatic. For a second, I almost don't recognize her. Her hair is tied back in a high, swishy ponytail, and she's wearing an emerald-green tracksuit top and huge dark-frame geek glasses.

"Ready to rock 'n' roll?" I ask Seth, who's standing beside me, staring at Clover's eccentric getup.

"Are you sure you need me?" Seth asks, looking a little pale. "I know you're just trying to help this Dominique girl and her brother, but I'm a brutal actor. What if we all get caught?"

"Seth, who's in the Mini with Clover?"

Seth peers into the car. "A D4 in full war paint?"

"Really?" I follow his gaze and see Amber Horsefell sitting behind Clover in the backseat. Now, that's a bit of a shocker. Clover was hoping to persuade one of the girls from the *Goss* to help her out today, but I guess they must have all been busy, so she roped Amber in instead. Amber is at Trinity College with Clover. They work on the college magazine, *Trinity Tatler,* together. Seth's right. She's a total D4.

"Clover must have been really desperate to ask her for help," I say. "But look again — who's sitting *next to* Clover?"

Seth's face lights up. "You didn't tell me Brains was part of Clover's crack crew."

I do jazz hands. "Surprise!"

Seth grins from ear to ear, the tips of which are turning bright pink. He loves Brains's band, the Golden Lions. Idolizes them, in fact.

"That's brilliant!" Suddenly he stops smiling. "But what will I say to him? The Lions are huge now. Brains is a superstar."

"He's still Brains. You've met him loads of times."

"I suppose," he says, but he doesn't sound all that convinced.

A blond woman with a long, pointy face like a greyhound's has pulled up behind Clover's Mini and is thumping her fist on the horn of her navy BMW. It's Renate Hamilton, Annabelle's mum, and the dark scowl on her face would suggest she's in a hurry and isn't happy that Clover's blocking her way.

"Come on, lads, jump in," Clover shouts over at us. "Someone's got her granny knickers in a twist."

Seth and I make a dash for the car as Clover starts singing, *"Heigh-ho, heigh-ho, it's off to work we go."* Before I've even gotten the door shut, Clover's roaring down the drive, leaving the still-glaring Mrs. Hamilton in the dust.

"So, team," Clover says, "everyone know what to do? Amber, do you remember your instructions?"

Amber nods seriously. "It shouldn't be a problem. I rang ahead to set up the interview, and I have lots of questions prepared on how to coach a winning Junior Cup team, thus delaying him for, like, at least ten minutes." She opens the notebook she's clutching on her lap. "He played for Ireland as a student, and he even wrote a sports column for *Trinity Tatler* when he studied at Trinity. We should find plenty to talk about."

Clover whistles. "I'm impressed, Amber. You've done your homework."

Amber smiles. "Thanks, Clover. I did my best." For a D4, Amber seems pretty clued in.

Clover nudges Brains with her elbow. "Brains? You coola boola with your role?"

He gives her a confident grin. "Cool as peppermint, babes. Do I look the part?" he asks, pushing his geek glasses up the bridge of his nose. Unlike Clover's, the glasses are actually his. On his head is a dark-green IRFU — Irish Rugby Football Union — cap that's struggling to contain his wild afro, and he's also wearing an emerald-green tracksuit, complete with identity tag around his neck. He studies the tag for a moment. "Nice piece of counterfeiting, if I do say so myself. All those years of churning out fake IDs has come in handy."

"What does it say?" I ask him.

"'Rambo Harrington. IRFU Drug Tester.'"

"Brains!" Clover squeals. "*Rambo?* What's wrong with Matt or Simon or something? Did you have to pick such an over-the-top name?"

"I thought all rugby players had funny names," he says. "Like Crusher and Doom."

"I think you'll find that's *Gladiators*, mate," Seth says. "Not rugby."

"Ah, right," Brains says.

Clover's eyes narrow. "So, what's the name on my tag, then? Break it to me gently."

Brains coughs a little while telling her, so I can't quite hear what he's saying.

Clover takes a deep breath and clutches the steering wheel so tightly that her knuckles go white. "Brains, tell me you did not just say what I think you just said. Because it's not funny. This is a serious business. Happo's heart is at stake, remember? And no one's going to believe that Mystique Moore is a proper name."

"Stop fretting," Brains says, patting her hand. "They won't even read the tags. They're Crombies, not MI6 spies. Chill, Mystique. Or should I call you Misty?"

Clover sets her jaw. "Still not funny."

But when Brains starts singing a weird song about misty moors and wuthering heights in a mad, high-pitched voice, we all fall around the place, laughing, even Clover. I think it's partly nerves.

"Hand Amy and Seth their costumes, please, Amber," Clover says when we've finally stopped laughing.

Seth and I are already wearing our navy school tracksuit bottoms, so we pull matching green hoodies, the same color as Brains's and Clover's, over our school shirts.

"Where did you get all this green sports gear?" I ask Clover.

She looks in the rearview mirror at me and pats her nose. "I *nose* people," she says with a smile. "Get it? Knows?"

"That's brutal, Clover." I groan and shake my head.

Clover parks to the far right of the Monkstown College changing rooms. We've timed our arrival perfectly. Happo's team has just finished its after-school training session and is walking off the field, followed by their coach — a surprisingly cute dark-haired man in his late twenties.

"Phew! Just in time," Clover says. "You're on, Amber. Break a leg, babes."

"Thanks." Amber springs into action. Climbing out of the car, she runs after the coach — which is pretty impressive considering her six-inch heels. They are part of her "cute reporter girl" outfit — red heels, white shirt with pussycat bow, and ultratight black pencil skirt, which makes her trot along like a show pony.

"Mr. Winters," she calls after the coach. "Excuse

me, Mr. Winters." She catches up with him and puts her hand on his thick, muddy forearm.

He stops and stares at her, looking confused. Amber introduces herself and asks if he's ready for the interview. He gives a toothy grin and nods enthusiastically. Then they walk off toward the main school building together. Without turning round, Amber twists her arm behind her back and gives a thumbs-up.

"Way to play it, Amber!" Clover says. "I knew she was the right girl for the job. She has a lot of smarts for a D4. And she certainly knows how to handle her heels. Ready, Operation Happo team? Thunderbirds are go, go, go! Let's show these Crombies we mean business. Follow me, troops." We all pile out of the car and head over to the changing-room door that Happo's team has just gone through.

As soon as we enter and start walking down the slightly gloomy hallway, I can smell the familiar odor of teenage boy — rancid socks, sweat, body spray, and hormones. There's shouting and laughter from behind a door, and Clover stops in front of it.

"This must be it," she says in a low voice. "Bean Machine, you're keeping watch outside the door. Seth, you're the bouncer. Don't let anyone inside the building, understand? As soon as you spot the coach or any other adult, wave at Amy, OK? And she can alert me and Brains."

"OK," Seth says, now looking as green as our hoodies.

"So are we all set, team?" Clover asks.

Seth and I nod. I have to admit, my stomach is knotted with nerves. Seth squeezes my hand. "Good luck, kiddo. See you on the other side."

"Stay alive," I gush while gripping his hand. "I will find you. No matter how long it takes, no matter how far, I will find you."

Clover frowns. "Beanie! This is no time for amateur dramatics. Right, it's action stations, troops."

I salute her. "Aye, aye, Captain."

Clover knocks loudly on the changing-room door, opens it a little, and shouts, "Lady incoming." After waiting a second or two, she strides in, with Brains just behind her.

Standing outside, I feel another wave of anxiety. What if the Crombies don't believe Clover and Brains are with the IRFU? They don't exactly look like your average rugby officials.

"Excuse me." Clover's voice cuts into my thoughts. The sound is carrying through the thin changing-room door. "Can I have your attention, please?" She sounds very confident and very, very official. "This is the Junior Cup team, is that correct?"

"Yeah," a voice rings out. Then there's a wolf whistle.

"Less of that now, please, lads." It's Brains this time, with a surprisingly brilliant accent. "We're here on important IRFU business. If we have your full cooperation, it won't take long."

"As you all know, the use of performance-enhancing drugs is banned in rugby, and we at the drug-testing unit take our jobs very seriously indeed," Clover says. "Now, as I'm sure you're all aware, random drug testing is part of any athlete's life, and the IRFU is following the Olympic officials' lead. So today we will be taking urine samples from two of your players and testing them for illegal substances."

"You can't just barge in here and do that without a warning," a boy says angrily. "My dad's a lawyer. I know these things."

"Actually, they can," another boy says. "My cousin's an Olympic swimmer, and she's tested all the time."

"What's your name, son?" Brains asks him.

"Happo," he says. "Sorry — Harry O'Loughlin."

Bingo!

"One of the names on my list, in fact," Clover says. "Would you mind going with Brai—sorry, Mr. Harrington—here and giving us a sample? As I said, the sooner we get the tests done, the sooner we can be out of your hair."

"Me?" Happo sounds nervous.

"Yes," Clover says firmly.

"Hey, shouldn't our coach be here for this?" the first boy asks.

"He's in the office, filling out the paperwork with our colleague, Ms. Moneypenny," Clover says smoothly. "So Harry first and then you, please."

"Why me?" another boy says.

"It's a random selection," Clover says. "And unless you are using steroids or any other performance enhancers, you have nothing to worry about. As of yet, creatine is not on the banned substance list, in case any of you are wondering. But steroids most certainly are." She pauses for a second and then adds, her voice grave, "Of course, you're all far too intelligent to go down that route, aren't you, boys? Because you know your entire rugby career would be over if you tested positive for steroids, right? Plus, your whole team would be thrown out of the league and banned from playing for three years. You wouldn't want that on your head, would you?"

The room goes deathly silent.

"So, if you'd do the honors, please, Mr. Harrington," Clover continues. "And then we can be on our way. And do tell any other rugby players you know about the dangers of using banned substances, boys. We might be testing their school soon. I think Saint John's is next on our list, in fact, along with Blackrock College and Saint Michael's. So, do spread the word."

"Success," Clover says as we walk back toward the car. "I think they're suitably terrified. There's no way Happo will touch steroids now."

"You were amazing, Clover," I say.

She grins. "I was rather good, wasn't I? And Brains did a stellar job with the sample jars and the food coloring. Rather you than me, babes. Yuckster!"

"All in the line of duty," Brains says. "But I sure am glad I was wearing two pairs of surgical gloves."

"No kidding," Clover says. "Now, where's Amber? We need to skedaddle, tout de suite."

Brains starts singing the "Toot Sweet" song from *Chitty Chitty Bang Bang,* and we all laugh. And this time it's not the nerves.

We're climbing back into the car when Amber reappears, smiling.

"Good interview?" Clover asks.

"Great! He was actually very interesting, for a rugby player."

Clover looks at her, surprised. "You're not into rugby players?"

"No way. They're, like, the worst dancers. Besides, I like a man with brains."

"Hey," Brains says. "That's me. And my moves are pretty genius too." He gyrates his hips and we all go into fits of laughter again.

Clover throws her arms around him and gives him a kiss. "I know, babes. And sorry, Amber, he's already taken. Now, let's banana split!"

# ♥ Chapter 13

Dear Clover and Amy,

Happo came home today and told me about a drug test they'd had. He said it really freaked the lads out and everyone's talking about it. The team captain has made them all swear they won't go near steroids, ever, for the sake of the team and the school's good name. "No glory if it's illegal glory, lads," he said, apparently. They're right drama queens in Monkstown College some- times. And the news is spreading like wildfire on Facebook. I hope it means all the rugby-playing schools will hear about it soon.

But here's something odd — the coach rang someone at the IRFU about the test, and they didn't know anything about it. They suggested it might be something to do with the department of health . . .

It was you guys behind that drug test, wasn't it? I have no idea how you pulled it off, but it worked. I owe you so much, girls. I don't know how to thank you. There are tears in my eyes as I type, I swear, I'm so grateful. I don't want to sound totally over-the-top and stuff, but you may have saved Happo's life.

Yours forever,

Dominique O'Loughlin

xxxxxxxxxxxxxxxxxxxxxxxxxxxxxxxxxxxxxxxxxxxxx
xxxxxxxxxxxxxxxxxxxxxxxxxxxxxxxxxxxxxxxxxxxxx
xxxxxxxxxxxxxxxxxxxxxxxxxxxxxxxxxxxxxxxxxxxxx
xxxxxxxxxxxxxxxxxxxxxxxxxxxxxxx + a trillion!

# ♥ Chapter 14

That evening I'm sitting in my room. I'm supposed to be reading *To Kill a Mockingbird* for school, but instead I'm thinking about Dominique's brother, Happo. I'm so happy we were able to help him and that my drug-testing idea worked. It was pretty inspired, if I do say so myself! Maybe I'm not such a bad person after all, despite what Mills thinks. After all, if Happo had listened to his teammates and taken steroids, he could have killed himself, and for what? A game! But I guess rugby is his passion, just like dancing is Claire's passion.

Hang on! If there are drugs that can make you gain weight, there must be drugs that can make you *lose* weight. Maybe Claire's taking something to help her slim down. Didn't her ballet teacher — that scary-sounding Madame Irina — call her fat and flabby? Maybe that's it! Maybe that's what's wrong with her. What if what she is taking is dangerous, like those steroid things? And what if I can help Claire, like I helped Happo? Would Mills forgive me then? It's a long shot, but it's got to be worth a chance. I know it's wrong to keep reading Claire's private thoughts, but if it saves her life . . . I just have to read more of her diary and find out if I'm right.

I open Claire's diary and start to read some of the entries, looking for clues, but they're all about how tough Madame Irina's classes are and how much Claire thinks she's improving, plus funny things Lana has said or done and how bad the food is at the academy. There's also the odd mention of how homesick Claire is, how much she misses Ireland and Mills and her parents and the food — she's obsessed with Irish butter, chocolate and crisps, and her mum's monthly junk-food parcels. Aha — junk food! Maybe she put on a lot of weight, couldn't lose it, and then resorted to some sort of drugs or diet pills and is now addicted. No wonder she's such a skinny Minnie.

Then I discover this entry:

Dear Diary,

Today we started duet classes, which meant we got to dance with the boys for the very first time — yeah! They all marched into the studio behind Madame Irina like they owned the place, tossing their heads and nudging one another. They reminded me of stallions, lean and strong and full of restless, wiry energy. I half expected them to start whinnying.

Zsuzsanna made a big deal of waving at one of them, a boy in a black T-shirt and shorts, with wide shoulders and curly dark-blond hair.

"Péter!" she called.

The boy raised his hand and grinned at her easily. When he smiled, his face lit up and his brown eyes twinkled. And his cheekbones — heaven! I had to drag my eyes away in case somebody noticed me staring at him. I'd seen him before in the cafeteria and wondered who he was, but I'd never been this close to him before.

Some of the girls here hook up with the boys to have flings and relationships, but I don't have time for that sort of thing. And I haven't been all that interested in any of the Hungarian boys, to be honest, until now. . . . Some of them have tried talking to me, but they come across as very serious and intense. This boy seems different, though: lively and fun, and more like Irish boys.

I can't believe Zsuzsanna knows him. I dislike Zsuzsanna even more now!

She's being increasingly nasty to me as the weeks go by. Last week she whispered to Nóra the whole way through my solo, and it was really off-putting. Madame snapped at her, and Zsuzsanna scowled at me, as if it was my fault! She hates the fact that people say I am better than she is. She thinks she's the best in the class. As if!

Anyway, at the start of the duet class, Madame Irina gave us another massive lecture about weight, in front of the boys and everything. She said that the boys couldn't be expected to lift any girl who is over 110 pounds. It would be too much of a strain on their bodies. She asked Lana to sit out. "We do not want any accidents," she told her.

At five foot eleven, Lana is one of the tallest girls in the class, and she's also the most muscular. I know she worries about her weight, but there isn't a bit of fat on her. You can see every bone of her rib cage pressing through her skin, like a ladder.

Lana went bright red.

Péter stepped forward then and said that he was strong and could lift any of the girls.

Madame wasn't impressed. She said that he could dance with Lana, but if he got injured, it was on his own head.

As there are twice as many girls as boys, the girls were broken into two groups and we took turns at being lifted. I was paired with a blond boy called Alexandr who's a good dancer with a safe pair of hands, but he isn't very exciting to watch or to dance with. He has no spirit. Not like Péter.

The boys have separate classes from ours normally, so I'd never seen Péter dance, but I'd heard about a guy called Péter who was amazing. As soon as I watched him dance, I understood immediately what all the fuss was about.

When Péter takes to the floor, everyone pays attention. It certainly isn't his technique, which can be a little sloppy and lazy. It's the sheer joy and passion he puts into every step. Every jump is higher, every leap wider. He's mesmerizing. And even when he lifted the tall girls like Lana, he made them look as light as feathers and as graceful as swans. He doesn't seem to realize how good he is either, which makes me like him even more.

At lunchtime, my head was still full of Péter, playing through his spectacular series of lifts in my mind. And, OK, I admit it, his beautiful face, his intense brown eyes, his strong, toned arms . . .

Lana got cross because I wasn't paying attention to what she was saying. I felt bad—she'd had a horrible morning. I noticed she wasn't eating her goulash.

"Madame said I have to drop seven pounds or I'm out of here," she said when I asked why.

I told her not to be so silly, that she needed the energy to dance, and besides, Péter had had no problem lifting her and they'd looked amazing together.

She gave a *pah,* but I could tell she was upset underneath her hard shell.

I'm worried about her. She needs to eat; otherwise she'll get sick. It's really unfair — Madame shouldn't put pressure on us to lose weight. No wonder some of the girls pick at their food.

Lana tried to change the subject by talking about the boys and saying how much fun it was to dance with them. I agreed, saying it was the best class ever. I told her I was jealous that she got to dance with Péter. And she said she thinks Péter likes me! Apparently he asked Lana about me after class. "You need to be careful," she said "'cause Zsuzsanna has her eye on him, and she'll be even nastier to you if Péter shows an interest."

I told her he probably just wants to practice his English or something, but secretly I'm thrilled. The best male dancer in the school, interested in me. Me!

I'm off to dream about Péter now, Diary. *Szia!*

xxx

That's more like it—romance a-go-go! Then I remember that from the look of things now, it has hardly ended in rainbows and lollipops for poor old Claire. Maybe Péter broke her heart? But there's nothing about Madame telling Claire specifically to lose weight or take any sort of drugs or diet supplements. I'm baffled. What *is* wrong with Claire Starr?

# ♥ Chapter 15

"What are you doing in, Amy?" Dave asks on Friday evening. I'm flopped in front of the telly, watching some incredibly tall and giraffe-legged Irish and English girls parade up and down a catwalk. "I thought you were going to Seth's house straight after school. Pizza and a movie — wasn't that what you said? I seem to remember giving you a tenner toward it too."

"Do you want it back?" I say, my eyes still glued to the screen. "Is that it?"

There's silence for a moment. Then I feel Dave's hand on my shoulder. I shrug it away.

"What's wrong, Amy? Want to talk about it?"

I shake my head.

"Might make you feel better," he says gently.

"I doubt it."

"Have you fallen out with Seth?"

I shake my head again.

"Mills?"

I know he's going to pick, pick, pick until it all comes out, or even worse, he'll fetch Mum to join in the interrogation, so I give in.

"Mills isn't speaking to me," I explain. "And before you say anything, there's nothing you or anyone else can do to fix it, OK? And no, I don't want to talk about it. She's over at Seth's place with Bailey. Seth was really looking forward to having people over, and I didn't want to cause any trouble, so I opted out. The end."

"I see." Dave blows out his breath in a *whoosh*. "Being a teenager sucks, doesn't it?"

I look at him, trying to work out if he's being sarcastic, but he seems sincere enough.

"I wouldn't go back to being thirteen for a million quid," he adds. "I'm sorry things are tough for you at the moment, Amy. But hang in there. It will get better, I promise."

"Thanks, Dave. I thought you were working this evening." Dave's a nurse, and he works all kinds of strange hours.

"Swapped shifts. Sylvie wants to talk about the wedding." He rolls his eyes at the word "talk," making me smile a bit.

"Do you want this room?" I ask.

"No, you stay put. We can have our chat in the kitchen." He leaves me to it and goes into the kitchen.

Bored with the program, I decide to follow him. Maybe wedding planning will improve my mood.

Dave and Mum are sitting at the kitchen table, dozens of magazine cuttings scattered in front of them. Mum's head is covered in paper towel, and she's giggling so hard that tears are running down her cheeks.

"What are you doing, Mum?" I ask her. "What's with the weird hat?"

Mum is laughing too much to speak, so she just waves her hand in front of her face.

"Your mum wanted to show me some of Clover's suggestions for her wedding dress," Dave says.

I wrinkle my nose. "A paper-towel hat?"

"In the magazine, it's Italian lace," Mum says, pointing at one of the cuttings, a photograph of a glamorous bride wearing what looks like a white, lacy nightie, with a matching mop cap on her head. "But it's so expensive, I thought I'd make my own."

"Your mum finds some of Clover's dress suggestions hilarious," Dave explains.

"Not to mention ridiculously priced," Mum

adds. "Look at this one. Almost ten thousand quid for a piece of old knitting. Are they crazy?" She points at a 1920s-style beige-crochet flapper dress with fringing along the hem that costs 9,750 euros, and a strapless Empire-line dress that's squashing the model's small breasts into a weird-looking tube shape that costs 6,500 euros.

"I could make that second dress out of one of Gramps's old tablecloths!" Mum says.

I smile at her. "It's early days, Mum, I'm sure you'll find something nice and not so expensive. Those are pretty." I point at some pearl-and-diamanté hair clips in the shape of large stars that are twinkling in a blond model's hair.

"You're right, Amy. They're beautiful," Mum says. "You have a good eye. In fact, that model's hair is perfect too, very natural."

There's a loud squawking noise from upstairs.

"Wanna play twains," comes a voice from the top of the stairs. "No go bed."

Alex.

Mum groans. "So much for our quiet evening in."

"I'll get him back to sleep," I say. "You guys stay here." It's nice to see Mum and Dave getting on so well. At least someone's having fun this evening.

\* \* \*

After settling Alex (which takes three Thomas the Tank Engine stories and two rounds of "Hush-a-Bye, Baby") and watching a bit more rubbish telly, I head upstairs to read in bed. I'm rereading an old copy of *The Sisterhood of the Traveling Pants* that used to belong to Clover. But I can't concentrate on the words. I keep wondering what Seth and Bailey and Mills are up to.

If I only had someone to talk to right now, maybe then I wouldn't feel so lonely. I don't like to bother Clover on a Friday night — she's bound to be out. Now, who can I ring? I think for a moment. Dad! He'll probably be in with Shelly and Gracie. I get up and find my iPhone, which is plugged into the laptop on my desk, recharging.

Dad answers immediately. "How weird. I was just about to ring you, Amy."

I feel a warm glow inside. At least someone's thinking of me!

"I wanted to ask you something," he says. "I caught Pauline checking out photos of some old dude in swimming trunks on Facebook earlier. And it's not the first time either. I think she's spying on him. Has Pauline ever said anything to you about having a boyfriend? I asked Shelly, but she said she didn't think so."

"Well, the dreaded Pauline was talking about

some man in Portugal when you and Shelly were putting Gracie back to bed the last time I was over. He's called Dean and he runs an Irish bar there."

"Dean? Just Dean? No surname?"

"I'm doing pretty well remembering that much. And why are you so interested in Pauline's love life? It's gross!"

"I was thinking I could track the man down and bribe him into dragging Pauline back to Portugal."

"Dad! That's terrible."

"I know, but I'm desperate, Amy. At this stage I'll try anything. I'm determined to stick it out till Christmas, but after that, it's either her or me."

After he rushes off to watch golf on the telly, I put my iPhone down. So much for someone to talk to. Did I really think Dad would have time for a proper conversation with me and listen to my problems for a change? And even if he does find this Dean guy, is he really going to bribe him into taking Pauline back to Portugal? Trust Dad to try to buy himself out of his problems again.

I wish I could ring Mills right now and tell her about Dad and his crazy plan, but I know I can't. And Seth wouldn't understand. He doesn't know Dad the way Mills does. Without my best friend to talk to, I feel so alone.

# ♥ Chapter 16

Dear Diary,

Well, it's finally happened. Madame Irina has driven Lana out of the academy, and I've lost the only friend I have in this godforsaken place. How am I going to cope? Zsuzsanna is already on my case. Without Lana to talk to, I don't know what I'll do.

I begged Lana to stay, but she was having none of it. She said she had to face facts. She's the wrong shape for ballet: too tall, too muscular. And she refuses to starve herself to lose weight, like some of the other girls. That is no life, she says. And she's right. Some of the girls here are on permanent diets, and it makes them miserable and grumpy all the time, and I'm sure some of them will get eating disorders.

I asked Lana what she was going to do instead. She shrugged and sighed and then her eyes went blurry. I've never seen Lana cry before, and it scared me. Then she blinked her tears back and stiffened her shoulders. She told me about her friend Miriam who runs a contemporary dance company back in Slovakia. She's offered her a place. "It's still dance, right?" Lana said. "And maybe later on I can teach." She gave me a smile, but it didn't reach her eyes.

I tried to be as enthusiastic as I could, but it was hard. Lana has always poked fun at modern dance and some of its jagged, angular movements. Then she told me not to worry about her. She'd be OK. "And do not let those Hungarian witches run *you* out, understand?" she said. "Swear to me?" I nodded, my stomach in knots at the thought of dealing with Zsuzsanna and Nóra alone.

After Lana left the academy, I cried my heart out. Afterward, I felt horribly guilty. I have no right to feel so sorry for myself. I'm still here, at one of the best ballet academies in the world. I still have the chance of being a prima ballerina, but Lana's ballet dreams have been crushed.

The next entry is dated a week later.

Dear Diary,

Class was hard today. I had no one to wink at when Madame Irina went off on one of her "You are all lazy, good-for-nothing shoe-shop girls, not dancers" rants. There was no one to help me perfect my steps after class, no one to translate what the teachers and the other girls were saying when they spoke too fast for me to understand — my Hungarian is getting better, but it's still not great. And no one to step in when Zsuzsanna gave me a hard time about dancing with "*my* partner," Péter, in duet class.

Before the lesson, Madame swapped everyone around and asked Péter to dance with just me. Zsuzsanna and Nóra both had to dance with Alexandr. Zsuzsanna protested wildly, but Madame told her to be quiet. Zsuzsanna and Nóra spent the rest of the class glaring at me as if I'd made the decision, not Madame. I love dancing with Péter. I know it sounds crazy, but I think we were born to dance together. I just wish it didn't cause so much aggro.

Yesterday Zsuzsanna kicked me several times during barre work. Her pointe shoe impacted so hard on my upper thigh that it left angry dark-purple marks. The first time she did it, I spun around and said, "Hey, watch your feet," thinking it was an accident. But by the third kick, I realized it was no accident. She wouldn't have

dared to do that if Lana was still around. But now I have
no one to stick up for me. And complaining to Madame
Irina will only make things worse.

So here I am, bruised body, bruised heart. How will
I survive without Lana? I have no friends here now, and I
feel so vulnerable and so alone . . .

I stop reading to wipe my tears away. I know
exactly how Claire feels. But at least I have my family and Seth to rely on, and I'm not being picked on
by anyone in school. There's Annabelle, I guess, but
compared to Zsuzsanna, she's a pussycat. Claire is utterly alone, and from the sound of things, she's being horribly bullied, both physically and mentally, by
this Zsuzsanna. If the bullying started in April of last
year, when this diary entry was written, then Claire's
had to deal with it for nearly two years. No wonder
she's cracking up. And I have no idea how to help her.

# ♥ Chapter 17

Dear Diary,
I'm bored, bored, bored, bored, bored, bored, bored, bored, bored, bored, bored, bored . . .

I snap my diary shut and fling it down on my bed. It's Saturday lunchtime and I'd usually be hanging out with Mills, checking out the shops in Dundrum, drinking megacreamy hot chocolates in Starbucks, or maybe catching a movie. Instead, I'm home alone. I flop down on my bed. I'm just perfecting a string of long, dramatic groans when Mum walks into my bedroom.

"Are you all right, Amy?" she asks. "You sound like you're in pain."

I feel my cheeks go pink. Why do mums always catch you doing embarrassing things, like practicing your groans?

"Just something for school. Shakespeare," I say.

She nods. Luckily most mums will also swallow anything. "Your dad's on the phone." She passes the home phone over and then stands there, waiting.

I look at her. She doesn't seem to have any intention of leaving. She's so nosy. "Ahem. Can I have some privacy please, Mother darling?"

I wait until I hear her footsteps on the stairs and then say, "Hi, Dad. What's up?"

He chuckles. "Sylvie trying to listen in again, eh?"

"She's obsessed with other people's business."

"Always has been. It comes with being a writer, apparently." Mum used to be a scriptwriter for an Irish soap opera called *Fair City*, but she gave it up when she had Evie. She still does some other bits of writing, but she's not working on anything at the moment.

"You can be quite nosy yourself, Dad," I point out. "Spying on Pauline and everything."

"Never say a word about that to anyone. Amy, promise me, especially not to Shelly. It was a stupid idea. Anyway, enough about my poisonous mother-in-law. What are you doing right now?"

"Why?" It sounds like a loaded question.

"Shelly has taken the witch into town for the afternoon to stop her moping around the house. It's a really nice day, and I was thinking I might be able to squeeze in a few holes."

"So you want me to babysit?"

He laughs. "Got it in one. And to sweeten the deal, I have something for you. I've just replaced our home laptop. I thought you could use our old one for your homework."

Homework? Facebook, more like! "Coola boola! Thanks, Dad. Of course I'll babysit. Although I would have done it anyway, even without the promise of a new laptop. Will you collect me or will I get Mum to drop me over?"

"Ah, well, here's the thing. Gracie's still very young. And you are only thirteen. So I was hoping you'd mind her there and that Sylvie might be around this afternoon in case—"

"In case I do anything stupid?" Charming!

"No, in case you need a hand. Babies are hard work, Amy."

"Dad, I know all about babies. I live with two of them, remember?"

"I know, pet, but it would make your old dad happy to know there was an adult on the premises."

"Oh, fine, I'll ask her. I'll ring you back in a minute."

"That's my girl. Thanks, Amy."

I click off the phone and walk out my door, nearly colliding with Mum, who has clearly been eavesdropping.

"*Siúcra*, Mum, you nearly gave me a heart attack."

"Sorry, but I knew Art was after something. He had that wheeler-dealer voice on. And I was right. He wants you to take Gracie off his hands so he can play golf, doesn't he? But only if I'm in the house so he doesn't feel too guilty about leaving a tiny baby in the care of a mere child."

God, she's good. I'm actually very impressed. Sleuthing must run in the family. "Child? Mother dearest, I'm thirteen. And haven't you watched any of those teen-mum programs on the telly?"

"What a terrifying thought, Amy," she snaps. "Don't even joke about things like that."

"I was kidding, Mother, please! What has you in such a bad mood all of a sudden?"

"Your father! He's always taking advantage of you, Amy, and it's just not fair. Why should you ruin your Saturday just because he wants to hit stupid little balls around with his fat, middle-aged banker mates?

Go on, ring him back and tell him you can't do it. Or would you like me to have a word with the man? I'd be only too happy to give him a piece of my mind."

"Mum, please let me babysit. It's the first time I've been allowed to mind Gracie on my own. She's my sister, and I want to help look after her. Give her a bottle, burp her, change her nappy, all that kind of stuff. Like I do with Alex and Evie." It's true, I really do want to get to know Gracie better. I'm going to be the best childminder and big sister ever.

Mum's eyes soften and she sighs. "Oh, Amy. How can I say no to that? Go on, then. Tell Art he can drop her off."

An hour later, Gracie is still asleep in her little baby chair and I'm sitting on the edge of my bed, staring down at her. I was hoping for lots of time playing together, singing her nursery rhymes and showing her some of Evie's toys, but she hasn't so much as opened her eyes yet. I rock her chair a little with my foot, but no, still nothing — just a funny-sounding hiccupy gurgle. Fabulous! Even my baby sister wants nothing to do with me.

Instead, I open the laptop Dad gave me. It's a top-of-the-range silver Sony. Nothing but the best for Dad. Mum nearly went crazy when she realized it was now mine. "You can't just give it to her, Art!" she'd said, almost apoplectic with rage. "How is Amy supposed to learn about the value of hard work when you hand over expensive gifts just like that? You should at least have waited till Christmas."

Dad had just shrugged. "What's the world coming to if I can't treat my daughter once in a while? Look, if it makes you happy, Sylvie, we'll call it an early Christmas present, OK?"

It didn't seem to make Mum any happier, but after more huffing and puffing, she eventually said I could keep it. And now it's sitting proudly on my desk. My very own laptop. How cool is that? Dad even set up the Internet and everything for me. While Gracie dozes, I switch it on and click on to Internet Explorer. Then I log in to my Facebook account and check for messages and updates. There are none. Mills was the only person who sent me messages on a regular basis, and now my page is depressingly quiet. I click on Mills's profile. Seeing her smiling head shot, complete with large heart-shaped sunglasses (her mum insisted on a Facebook "disguise"), makes me sad.

Out of curiosity, and to stop thinking about Mills, I load up Pauline's page. She hasn't set her privacy settings to "friends only," so I am able to flip through her photographs. There are lots of Pauline, Shelly, and baby Gracie at Gracie's christening and then some of Pauline playing cards with Dean. Pauline is beaming at the camera, her huge teeth glinting in the sunlight. She looks really happy. I realize with a start that I've rarely seen her smile. She must be really miserable in Ireland, away from the sun and away from Dean. She's obviously still crazy about the man, but she's too stubborn to tell him how she really feels.

And then I have a thought. What if there was a way of getting Pauline and Dean back together again and helping Dad out in the process? Surely a wee touch of undercover false-identity meddling wouldn't be wrong if it made people happy? The edges of my lips start to curl. I think I can feel another plan coming on . . .

# ♥ Chapter 18

On Monday morning, I'm walking toward the art building with Seth when I spot Bailey standing in front of the school notice board, peering at the rugby news. Dominique was right: word of the "Monkstown drug bust," as everyone's calling it, is all over the school, and hopefully it will nip firmly in the bud any thoughts Bailey has of bulking up illegally.

"Hey, Bailey," I say as we walk toward him.

"Hey, guys. How goes it, Greenster? Long time no see."

"OK," I say. It's all a bit awkward. I haven't talked to Bailey properly for days. I know he's Mills's boyfriend and everything, but we're supposed to be friends too. But right now we're just standing here, staring at each other, as if we're strangers.

"Better get to class, kiddo," Seth says gently and puts his hand on my arm. "Don't want to be late for Olen. See you later, Bailey." Mr. Olen's our art teacher, and he can be as moody as the Irish weather, all sunny smiles one day, gray growls the next.

"You go on, Seth," I say. "I just want to talk to Bailey for a second."

Seth looks at me, his eyes soft, and then says, "Will do." That's what I love about Seth. He knows I'm having a rough time at the moment, what with Mills and everything, and he's being so sweet. Seth's thoughtful behavior makes falling out with Mills almost worth it. Only almost, though, 'cause, let's face it, having a best friend, someone who truly understands and accepts you, warts and all, is what makes life bearable. Without Mills, I feel like someone's lopped my right arm off.

But as Clover and Seth have both pointed out, it's not forever; she's bound to change her mind at some point. After all, we've fallen out before — like when I "forgot" to tell her about getting together with Seth last spring, and she got all pally with Sophie (who used to be friends with both of us before she turned D4) and dumped me — but we've always made up. And we will this time, I'm sure. At least I hope we will. She has to forgive me eventually, doesn't she?

I look at Bailey, biting my lip nervously. He seems equally uneasy. I think he suspects what's coming.

I take a deep breath. "Sorry, Bailey. I know you probably don't want to get involved, but this whole thing with Mills is really getting to me. It's been days now, and I miss her desperately. I just want things to go back to normal. I know I hurt her, and I'm really, really sorry. I'll do anything to get her back. Will you tell her that? Tell her how sorry I am and how awful I feel about upsetting her. Please?"

Bailey takes a few seconds to answer. "I miss you too, Greenster. It wasn't the same on Friday night without you."

"Does Mills miss me?" I ask eagerly.

His face falls a little.

"You don't have to answer that," I say. "But surely she's softening up a bit? She's going to change her mind eventually, right? We've been best friends for years."

"It's not looking good," Bailey says slowly. "She's pretty—" He stops abruptly and sighs. "Look, it's probably best just to let her be for the moment. She can be kinda stubborn."

"Tell me about it. So you're saying I just have to wait around and hope for the best?"

He shrugs. "I guess. I'm sorry. I've tried reasoning

with her, but she's still mega-upset. Seth tried talking to her about everything on Friday night and she yelled at him and then started crying."

I wince. That doesn't sound like Mills at all. The crying bit, yes; the yelling, no. She must still be seriously angry. "Thanks for trying, Bailey."

He gives me a gentle smile. "'S OK. I hope she does change her mind. She needs you just as much as you need her. Take care of yourself, you hear?"

I nod and walk away so that he doesn't spot the tears that have started to spill down my cheeks.

That evening, I'm sitting at my desk, trying to do my homework, but my mind is racing. I can't stop thinking about Bailey and how together he seemed today. A few months ago, he was in a pretty dark place, doing badly at school and lashing out at everyone who cared about him. He's had a difficult past. His mum was bringing him up on her own, but she couldn't cope, and she abandoned him when he was a toddler. When his father, Finn, finally found out what had happened and got in touch with him, Bailey was a teenager and didn't want anything to do with him. Bailey felt that, as Finn hadn't been around when he'd really needed a father, why should he talk to Finn now? But eventually Bailey realized that the more people you have in your life who care about you, the better, so he forgave Finn and now they live together.

Mills has been brilliant for Bailey. She's always been his biggest fan, and I'm sure she's part of the reason that he's doing so well now. Soon after they got together for the first time, he pushed her and everyone else away. Mills was devastated, but they made it up and now they're inseparable. She's a brilliant girlfriend and a brilliant friend, and I should never have dissed her like that in my diary. What was I thinking? I keep going over and over it in my head, how one stupid action can have so many consequences. Writing about Mills was like throwing a stone in the sea and not realizing the ripples it would cause.

And like Bailey, I *need* Mills too. I need her horribly. But maybe this time it's different. Maybe Mills really has moved on. How will I cope with school? How will I cope with life?

"How's the homework going, Amy?" Mum asks, walking into my room.

"I think I'm sick," I lie. "I feel all hot and feverish. Maybe I've got one of those virus things. I don't think I should go to school tomorrow."

"Your cheeks are a little flushed," Mum says, putting a hand against my forehead. "And you are quite hot. I'll get Dave to take a look at you. He'll be home soon."

I blush. I know Dave will find nothing wrong with me. Luckily Mum doesn't seem to notice my red face, although she does sit down on my bed with a funny look in her eyes. Oh, no, not a serious chat. Please not that, not right now! I start to feel as prickly as a hedgehog.

"Is there something else bothering you, Amy?" she asks. "Is it Mills? I bumped into Sue this morning in the supermarket, and she said you two still weren't talking."

"As Sue Big-mouth Starr seems to have filled you in, I don't need to answer that, do I?"

"There's no need to snap, Amy. I'm only trying to help."

"Well, don't. There's nothing you can do. Mills hates me."

"I'm sure she doesn't hate you. 'Hate' is a very strong word. Friendships are difficult sometimes. And you have to work at them."

"You're not helping, Mum."

"Sorry. But I'm sure she'll come around. And I have something that might cheer you up. I was going to give it to you after your homework, but you can have it now." And she hands over a magazine.

I instantly recognize the face smiling out from the front cover. It's Claire Starr, her dark hair scraped back in a high ballerina bun, the sides plaited with thin white ribbon. She's wearing a simple white-chiffon dress, and she looks stunning.

"Clover dropped this off earlier," Mum says. "It's a great piece. She's a clever writer, that sister of mine, I'll give her that."

Mum's only trying to be nice, and I shouldn't be taking my feelings out on her, so to make up for it, I say, "You're a great writer too, Mum. It must run in the family."

She smiles. "Thank you, Amy. That's a nice thing to say. You can have a break to read Clover's article. Then, when you're feeling a little better, it's back to your homework. Deal?"

"Deal." I flip open the magazine before Mum has a chance to change her mind.

"Try to stay positive, Amy," she says. "Time is a great healer."

"Mum! I'm trying to read."

"OK, OK, I'm going, I'm going. I'm glad you seem to have perked up a bit. Oh, and Clover said to ring her once you've finished reading the article. You know my sis, a total praise monkey."

"Will do." Any excuse to ring Clover.

I find Clover's interview near the front of the *Goss*. A whole three pages of it too! I start to read:

## A STARR IN THE MAKING
## CLOVER M. WILDGUST MEETS CLAIRE STARR, THE IRISH BALLERINA

Claire Starr is a name you'd better start getting used to hearing. This megatalented Irish seventeen-year-old is about to set the stage of the Bord Gáis Energy Theatre alight with her stirring rendition of Juliet. Watch out, world, there's a new Starr on the horizon. But where did Claire get her amazing talent, and what drives her? The *Goss* sent its own rising star, Clover M. Wildgust, behind the scenes to find out . . .

Ireland is not known for its ballerinas. Apart from Ninette de Valois, who set up the famous Sadler's Wells Ballet in London, and Monica Loughman, who danced with the Perm Ballet and now has her own ballet company in Dublin, few Irish dancers have hit the headlines. But Claire Starr is set to change all that. And like both Loughman and de Valois, she started young.

"I've been dancing since I was tiny," Claire tells me from her family home in Glenageary, Co. Dublin.

"I was always skipping and jigging around the house, and Mum thought I'd like ballet, so she enrolled me in Miss Smitten's School of Dance when I was three. I loved it from the very first day. And then in February 2010, Miss Smitten heard that the Budapest Ballet Company was in Dublin auditioning for students. She thought I was ready, so she put me forward. And the rest is history."

I read on, fascinated. Although I know Claire's background better than almost anyone, Clover still manages to make it interesting. Mum's right, she's a really good writer. Clover goes on to ask Claire about Budapest and the academy, information I already know from reading Claire's diary, of course. Claire tells Clover about the journey from pupil to soloist, about the tough classes and the demands that ballet puts on dancers' bodies. It's all fairly upbeat, but toward the end of the interview, the tone changes a little.

So what's in the future for this extraordinary girl? And what roles would she like to dance?

"Definitely the Sugar Plum Fairy in *The Nutcracker*," Claire says with a smile. "It was the first ballet I ever watched live as a child. Mum took me for my birthday when I was eight, and I've never forgotten it. And Giselle, obviously. And Odette-Odile, the white swan and the black swan, in *Swan Lake*. That's an amazing role. As for the future, I'm just not sure. It will depend on a lot of things. Don't get me wrong, I love dancing, but I miss home a lot, and it's a tough world. You have to fight both physically and mentally to stay on top. Will I still be dancing in five, ten, fifteen years' time? To be honest, I just don't know."

Hopefully Claire Starr will continue to dance for many years to come. She's just too good not to. And maybe after that, she will teach a new generation of young Irish dancers by setting up her own ballet school in Dublin, like Monica Loughman. But one thing is for sure: the Irish Ballerina's debut as Juliet is not to be missed!

I put the magazine down on my desk and sit back in my chair. I give a low whistle. That's a pretty honest interview. Claire is definitely having second thoughts about her ballet career. And I'm almost positive it's all because of Zsuzsanna and the bullying. I can't keep the information to myself any longer. I have to tell someone. Claire's ballet career is at stake. Luckily, there's someone I can tell who will understand instantly, someone who (I hope!) won't judge me for reading Claire's diary in the first place. I pick up my iPhone and ring Clover.

"Y'ello?" she says brightly. "You are speaking to the rising star of the magazine world. How can I be of assistance?"

"Fabarooney interview, Clover. Best yet. Even Mum's impressed."

"It's pretty spectacular, isn't it? And Saffy digs it with a capital *D*. I've never heard the woman gush before, but gush she did, like a fountain. In fact, she loved the piece so much, she's asked me to do a follow-up interview. She wants me to find out more about Claire's life in Budapest and the 'grueling reality of a dancer's life,' triggered by Claire's confession that she might give it all up someday soon, which I have to admit I also found pretty shocking, as I told you before. I still wish I could help her. There was definitely something on her mind on the day of the interview."

I already knew I had to tell Clover about Claire's diary, but thankfully she's just given me the perfect in! I take a deep breath and before I can chicken out say quickly, "I think I know what's wrong with Claire . . . She's being bullied."

"*Bullied?* Seriously? How do you know that, Beanie? Did Claire say something to Mills about it?"

"No, I read Claire's diary."

"*What?* I don't understand."

I tell Clover exactly what happened: how I stumbled on Claire's diary while she was home for the prepublicity tour, and how I made a copy and then read it. I explain what I've discovered about Zsuzsanna and the kick marks. As I talk, I can feel my cheeks burning with shame.

"I know it was a terrible thing to do," I say finally. "Reading someone's private thoughts like that is unforgivable. But I didn't feel I had any other choice. Claire is so obviously in pain, and I want to help her."

There's silence for a few seconds and I wait in agony for Clover to say something.

Eventually she sighs. "Sometimes life is complicated, Beanie, that's for sure. No, you shouldn't have read Claire's diary. It was one hundred percent wrong, but I can tell you're genuinely worried about her, and I think you have every reason to be. So in this case, I guess maybe the end justifies the means."

"So you're not disappointed in me for stealing her diary and reading it?" I feel almost dizzy with relief.

"No, Beans. I probably would have done exactly the same thing if I'd been in your shoes. And if I know you, you're probably already beating yourself up about it every single day. Am I right?"

"Yes," I admit. "*Serious* guilt pangs."

"And that's just something you're going to have to live with, I'm afraid. But this does make my next piece of news rather interesting for both of us. Saffy's flying me out to Budapest to talk to Claire. My darling editor wants me to hang out with Claire for a day, watch a *Romeo and Juliet* rehearsal, get a feel for where she lives, what she eats, what the other dancers are like — that kind of thing. Plus, I have to organize a couple of photo shoots. We're getting an amazing response to my first interview with Claire, and Saffy's itching to make the next interview another cover story. She's putting me up in a swanky boutique hotel and everything. And, boy, am I hungry for Hungary."

I laugh. "That's terrible, Clover. The joke, I mean. But it's fantastic news, and you really deserve it. You rocked that interview."

"I did, didn't I?"

"And maybe you can get Claire to open up about the bullying. Encourage her to talk to someone, get some help."

"Ah, that's where my second piece of news comes in. Are you sitting down, Green Bean? I talked to Sylvie earlier and . . . you're coming to Budapest with me! So we can talk to Claire together."

I squeal. "Are you serious, Clover?"

"*Absolument*, babes. Would your old aunt lie to you? The tickets are already booked. We're leaving Friday late afternoon for two nights of ballet balhooey in Budapest."

I still don't quite believe it. "Are you sure Mum said yes?"

"I talked her around. But you so owe me one, Beanie."

"I owe you a lot more than one, Clover. Can we do the whole touristy thing? Visit the art gallery? I haven't had a proper art fix for ages. And I'm sure there are castles, and museums and . . ." The line's gone quiet. "Clover? Are you still there?"

"You're joking, right? Culture, smulture. Not this trip, babes, sorry! You've got the wrong girl. I intend to eat, drink, and be merry. Oh, and have a good old soak in one of the famous baths. . . . Oops, Brains is on the other line. Better boogie. I'll talk to you tomorrow. And no guidebook studying, OK? Promise? I don't want any lectures on Hungarian history on the plane."

I cross my fingers. "Promise."

I click off my iPhone, a big grin on my face. Budapest! With Clover! And only four more sleeps!

# ♥ Chapter 19

"Nothing's going to happen, Beanie," Clover says as we take our seats in the blue Aircoach bus. "Stop being such a worrywart."

"You say that, but something always goes wrong. On the way to Paris, you forgot your passport and Gramps had to tear up the M50 to give it to you. On the way to Miami, we nearly missed our flight 'cause you were trying on posh sunglasses. When it comes to traveling, you're jinxed."

"Not this time, babes," she says confidently. "My passport's safely in my handbag, along with the tickets, my laptop, and thousands of florints." She pats the chic tan Alexa satchel, "borrowed" from the *Goss*'s fashion wardrobe especially for the occasion.

"*Thousands* of florints? Are we rich?"

"Don't get too excited. There are about three hundred florints to a euro. It's for our expenses. And that does not include icky, cheap, plastic models of Hungarian castles."

"Boo!" I say. Clover knows I love touristy things, the tackier the better. "So how long is the flight?" I ask.

"Just under three hours."

"And will you be snoozing, snoring, and drooling as usual?"

"I do not snore or drool, Beanie. How dare you!"

I smile to myself. She *so* does.

Sure enough, halfway over England, Clover is already sounding like a Great Dane with an adenoids problem. She's snoring seriously loudly. Comedy loudly. Everyone's staring at her, and they don't look happy. I'd better do something. After taking out my iPhone, I stick it in front of her open mouth and make a short sound recording. Then I shake her arm. "Wakey wakey, Sleeping Beauty."

She gives one last shuddery snort, then peels her eyes open slowly, one by one. "What? Are we there?"

I shake my head. "Some of the passengers are starting to get seriously worried. They think there's a farmyard animal on board."

I press "play" on my mobile, and her slobbery snores ring out.

"Beanie!" she cries. "That's disgusting. That can't be me."

"It is, Miss Snuffleupagus."

"Maybe I have a bit of a cold or something. I don't normally snore, you know."

I try not to laugh.

"You'll have to keep me awake, just in case," she says huffily. "Tell me some interesting facts about Budapest. I know you've been secretly reading that travel guide you've sneaked into your backpack."

I love travel guides, especially glossy ones with lots of photographs. I like to know a bit about the history of a place before I visit. Clover thinks it's boring, but Mum says that's because Clover's mind is a cultural black hole and her idea of history is last year's *X Factor*.

I pull out my guide eagerly and flip through the pages. "Did you know that Budapest is often described as the Paris of Middle Europe? Or that there are over sixty galleries and museums in the city?"

Clover groans. "Jeez Louise, Beanie, I said *interesting*, not snooze-inducing. You're supposed to be keeping me awake, not boring me into oblivion. I'll read my magazine instead." She picks up her handbag, which is under the seat in front of her, and rummages through it without success. "Must be in my wheelie bag." She stands up and opens the overhead bin. Then she looks back at me. "Beanie, where did you put my wheelie bag?"

"Last time I saw it was on the Aircoach. You put it in the trunk, remember? Mine fit under the seats, but yours didn't."

She screws her eyes tightly shut and then opens them again. "Oops!"

"Clover, you look blingtastic," I say, stifling my giggles. "Just like a gangsta rapper's moll." Clover is standing in front of me in a knee-length flamingo-pink Puffa jacket with a halo of fluffy white fake fur around the hood. Her feet are snug in matching silver-and-pink puffy snow boots. We're in the only clothes and shoe shop at Budapest airport, and it's pretty slim pickings. But as it's minus two degrees outside and Clover has only a light leather jacket, a red knitted skater dress, and ballet flats to her name, she doesn't have much choice. She has to buy them, along with some lacy black underwear, black jeggings, and two sequin-encrusted purple tops. I offered to lend her some of my clothes, but she said there was no way she'd fit into them. "I'm far curvier than you, babes," she said. "Your jeans would cut off the circulation in my legs."

She studies herself in the shop mirror. "At least no one I know is going to see me over here. I'm such a muppet. I spent a whole night sorting out my Hungarian wardrobe too."

While she's paying, I adjust my own bag on my shoulder and look out into the foyer, past the scurrying travelers, toward the doors leading outside. I can see what look like white feathers falling from the sky, spinning in the orange airport lights. "Look, Clover. It's snowing."

She grins. "You'd better pull on your beanie, Beanie. It's snow time."

Outside, I stick my tongue out to catch the swirling flakes. They melt instantly.

Clover laughs. "You're such a child, Bean Machine."

"At least I don't look like a skiing Bratz doll."

"Touché, darling." And then she pelts me right in the face with a snowball.


The hotel is amazing! I wasn't sure what to make of it at first. The taxi driver drove up all these narrow rickety streets and then dropped us off outside a huge wooden door with a curved top. There is a small brass plaque outside saying BALZAC HOUSE. Clover pressed the intercom. There was a buzzing noise and the lock on the door clicked open, but no one came to meet us. We looked at each other, shrugged, and then walked inside.

The hallway is spectacular. It has huge, soaring vaulted ceilings, like the inside of a Victorian church, and it smells like a church too, of old wood and damp.

As we stood there wondering what to do next, Clover wrinkled her nose. "Bit smelly." But as soon as she spotted a tall, beautifully dressed Hungarian man in his early twenties walking down the sweeping marble staircase toward us, a welcoming smile on his handsome chiseled face, she quickly changed her tune. "Now, that's more like it," she murmured.

"Welcome to Balzac House," he said politely in perfect English. "Can I take your bags?"

"I wish you could," Clover said wistfully.

He looked confused.

"Clover's bag got lost on the way," I explained.

He shook his head. "That is a shame. Airlines. So disorganized."

Before I could correct him, Clover had pressed her foot against mine and grinned. I smiled back at her.

"I will arrange a welcome pack for you—

toothpaste, shampoo, et cetera," he continued. "Is there anything else I can do to help?"

"Not at all. You're a complete doll," Clover said. "But if I think of anything, I'll be sure to let you know."

"Let me carry those." He took my bag and backpack from me. "I hope you will enjoy your stay," he said, leading us up the stairs.

"You're such a sweetie," Clover gushed, her eyes fixed firmly on his bum. "We definitely will," she added, wiggling her eyebrows and digging me in the ribs. I could only laugh.

I'm now lying on the double bed, waiting for Clover to come out of the bathroom. She's been in there for ages. I had a quick shower, but she insisted on filling the giant old-fashioned brass bath and having a soak in all the delicious smelly things that the hotel provided. The receptionist also dropped off a large plastic bag packed with toiletries, so she's really happy.

I'm starting to get bored. "Clover, hurry up. I'm starving," I shout at the bathroom door.

Nothing.

"Clover? You OK?"

I hear a splash and then, "Sorry, Beanie. Must have drifted off. How long have I been in here?"

"Too long. Get your skates on. My stomach is growling like a grizzly."

Seconds later she appears in the doorway, cheeks bright red and shiny from the bath. "Give me two secs."

I avert my eyes as she dashes past me, completely naked. "Clover!" I say.

She just laughs. After shimmying into her underwear, she starts doing this funny hula-hula dance, wiggling her hips, waving her arms in the air, and singing, *"I love ma body. I love ma body."*

"Have you completely lost the plot? Get dressed. You'll freeze."

"It's only skin, Beanie. We all have it. And I happen to love the skin I'm in."

Outside, it's a beautiful night — clear, crisp, and freezing. Our breath hangs in the air like little dragon puffs. The city is gorgeous, and it is a little like Paris, with its old buildings and pretty squares. It seems edgier, though, as if anything could be lurking around the next corner.

We head toward Vörösmarty Square. When we asked Boris, the receptionist from the hotel — Clover shamelessly asked him his name — where to go for dinner, he suggested we pick up some food at the famous Christmas Fair in the square and gave us directions. He promised it was only a few minutes' walk and was well worth the effort.

"I love this place," Clover says, swinging her arms and crunching through the fresh snow in her new boots. "It's got character. And I guess we've found the Christmas Fair." She points across the road at the dozens of brightly lit stalls.

As we cross the street, I smell mulled wine. It reminds me of Christmas Eve. Every year, Dad used to make a big saucepan of it for his and Mum's Christmas Eve party. I feel a slight tug in my stomach, thinking about Dad and Mum together. Yes, they argued a lot, but we were still a family. And now they both have different families, but I'm the bridge that links them together, and at the moment, I'm doing my best to *keep* Dad with his new family! So far, my Send-Pauline-Packing plan is coming along nicely.

We find a pancake stall and buy two savory pancakes, stuffed with gooey melted cheese and spicy sausage, and sit on white metal chairs under an outdoor heater to eat them while we watch the crowd mill by. Lots of the women are wearing coats just like Clover's. Others are wearing fur from top to toe, with big furry hats like cats perched on their heads.

After we've eaten, we wander among the stalls.

Clover munches on some roasted chestnuts. I try one, but they don't really taste of anything and they leave a funny zingy aftertaste in my mouth, so one is enough. Then I spot a tourist stall and I'm like a bee drawn to honey.

"Oh, no," Clover says, trying to drag me past it.

But I give her my best puppy-dog eyes. "Pwetty pwease?" I beg her.

She sighs. "Just a quick look."

I spot a snow globe with a tiny ballerina perched on her tippy-toes in it. It's perfect for Mills. Then I remember that she's not exactly speaking to me at the moment. But I buy it anyway.

As we make our way back to the hotel, the snow starts falling thick and fast, covering the footpath with a layer of what looks like fresh icing sugar. By the time we get to Balzac House, it's a couple of inches thick.

Clover throws herself on the ground and moves her arms up and down. "Snow angels. Come on, Beanie."

So, laughing, I lie down beside her, snow falling on my face, and make a snow angel too.

The perfect end to a perfect day.

Clover has another bath before bed, just because she can. I tell her she's going to shrivel up like a prune, but she says she doesn't care. "I never have time for a bath at home. Hotels are for pampering yourself, Beanie. And the best thing is, you don't even have to clean up afterward." With the mess Clover makes when she stays over at our house, sloshing bubbles all over the floor, it's probably just as well.

"Clover, can I use your laptop? I want to finish reading Claire's diary before we see her tomorrow."

There's a slight pause. "If you think it would be helpful, Beanie, then sure, fire ahead. In for a penny, in for a pound, and all that. Let me know if you find out anything else about the bullying."

So while she drifts away to bathe, I flip through the rest of Claire's diary entries. Most of them are short and more factual, and she doesn't mention Zsuzsanna again until the final entry. It was written just before she traveled to Dublin two weeks ago.

Dear Diary,

I wish things were different. I wish I could dance without worrying myself sick about everyone's reaction. I wish I could be with Péter properly, as his girlfriend, not just his friend. I wish I didn't feel the weight of this whole Irish production on my shoulders. But most of all, I wish Zsuzsanna would leave me the hell alone and stop tormenting me. The kicking, the hair pulling, the pushing in the corridors, the constant whispers and nasty rumors — it's driving me crazy!

I can't go on like this. It's destroying me. I used to be so strong and self-confident, and now look at me. I'm a nervous wreck! I have no nails because I've bitten them so much, and there are huge black bags under my eyes. I look ancient, not seventeen! Why is Zsuzsanna doing this? Why does she hate me so much? All I ever wanted to do was dance. It's not fair!

Am I even good enough to dance Juliet? Or to be in the company at all? I'm starting to seriously doubt myself. Zsuzsanna has told everyone that I was picked to be the lead just because I'm Irish and it will please the home crowd. She says I'm not up to the role and she should be dancing Juliet instead. Péter keeps telling me that Zsuzsanna's jealous and to pay no attention, but what if she's right? What if I'm not up to it? What if I make a complete fool of myself on the Dublin stage? I'll die!!!

I'm in such a state about everything that I can't eat or sleep. I really need to talk to someone, but Lana's gone and I can't say anything to Mills or Mum or Dad. They wouldn't understand. I've told Péter about my nerves but not about Zsuzsanna. If she knew I was telling tales behind her back, she'd have even more reason to hate me.

If it wasn't for Péter and his encouragement, I think I would have backed out of dancing Juliet weeks ago. Maybe I should just let Zsuzsanna have the role, as she seems to want it so badly. Maybe then she'd get off my back and just leave me be.

I can't bear to think of a life without ballet, but as with Lana, maybe it's just not for me. I thought I was strong enough, but what if I was wrong? Maybe Juliet will be my swan song. I'll dance Juliet and then . . . and then . . .

The writing stops abruptly. I peel my eyes from the screen. My heart is beating fast. Claire sounds like she's in such distress, and I desperately want to help her. She can't stop dancing. She just can't! She's too good, and she's worked too hard to throw it all away.

Originally maybe I was hoping that if I fixed things for Claire, Mills might forgive me, but it has gone way past all that now. If the bullying doesn't stop, if it continues to grind Claire into the ground and she's forced to throw away the one thing she loves most in the whole wide world, then what? I dread to think. I can't let that happen. I have to help her, but how?

# ♥ Chapter 20

"Now, that is a stunning swimsuit," I say. "It really suits you." I'm trying to keep a straight face, but it's difficult. Clover is standing in front of me in the weirdest swimsuit I've ever seen. It's fluorescent orange and slashed to the belly button. A large gold ring holds together the two thin strips of fabric covering Clover's breasts. It was that or a leopard-skin microbikini. The shop in the baths wasn't exactly well stocked.

We're in the Gellért Baths, housed in a huge old gray hotel on the side of Gellért Hill, and it's pretty chic in an Addams Family kind of way: murky, with lots of big ferny potted plants, stained-glass windows, and funny little stairways leading off the main hall. The changing rooms are pretty normal, though:

clammy tiled floors and lots of primary colors, like in a nursery school.

We're here for the photo shoot that Clover set up for Claire and some of the other dancers. Saffy wants some interesting photos in an "exotic" Hungarian location, and the baths with their aquamarine tiles, gold pillars, and palm trees are certainly exotic.

Clover puts her hands on her hips and pouts. "Why, thank you, darling. I hope the ballerinas appreciate it. To be honest, I'm spitting mad. I found this amazing white Chanel one-piece in the fashion cupboard. Beautifully cut. What a waste! I hope Sylvie managed to find my bag." Clover rang Mum yesterday and asked her to track down the missing wheelie case. Mum promised to do her best, but we haven't heard anything from her yet.

After locking up our changing rooms, we walk out into the deliciously warm air of the baths. "Race you," Clover says, running toward the palm-lined central swimming pool. She cannonballs in, making a big splash. Several old men mutter and wave their arms in protest at the lifeguard, a dark-haired boy of about eighteen. The lifeguard starts yabbering crossly at her in Hungarian.

Clover shakes the water off her head and gives him a big smile. "So sorry," she says. "Do forgive me, to be sure, to be sure. I'm Irish, ya see. We don't have baths like this in Ireland. Just wee concrete puddles that we have to share with the leprechauns and the donkeys. Tragic, really."

He looks at her crookedly as though trying to make out if she's serious. She gives him another wide smile, and this time he smiles back. "No jumping, OK?" he says. "Just swimming."

"I'll *tóg go bog é*, I promise." Clover gives him a big wink and a thumbs-up, and he wanders back to his plastic chair, looking confused.

I use the tiled steps to walk slowly into the pool until the water's up to my waist. It's not exactly warm and I shiver a little before forcing myself to get fully immersed, and then I swim toward Clover.

"Clover, you nearly got us thrown out," I tell her. "And what does '*tóg go bog é*' mean?"

She grins. "'Take it easy.' Do you not listen in Irish class, Beanie? And it was *so* worth it. Now let's explore before Roland and the girls arrive." Roland is the Hungarian photographer. It was cheaper to hire him here than to fly someone over.

As we swim back toward the steps, a tall, dark-haired girl lifts her leg in the water and places it on the edge of the pool. Then she leans forward slowly until her head is touching her knee.

"Must be a dancer," Clover whispers. "Claire says they come here a lot to relax and stretch."

We climb out of the pool and stand on the edge for a few seconds, dripping water onto the tiles.

"Ready for something a little more hot and steamy, Bean Machine?" Clover asks. She points at a doorway.

I nod. "Sure."

I follow her down a short corridor and through another arched doorway. Beyond, there are two large pools, steam wafting off both of them. Women of all shapes, sizes, and ages are draped about on marble seats and benches. Most of them are completely naked! I blush deeply.

"Are you sure we're supposed to be in here, Clover?"

"We're women, aren't we?"

"Speak for yourself. I'm only thirteen, remember? All this uncovered flesh is freaking me out. Can we go back to the other pool? Please?"

"Just one quick dip, Beanie. We may never be in Budapest again, and this is part of the whole experience. Be brave, Baby Bean. Come on."

So I follow her into one of the pools. It's swelteringly hot, but it feels surprisingly good. We wade toward one of the walls and sit on the smooth marble seat under a steady flow of warm water, letting it pour deliciously on our necks and backs. I close my eyes so I don't have to see any of the naked ladies.

"That's so good," Clover purrs. "The water's full of mineral salts. Very good for the skin, according to Saffy. She's obsessed with her skin. She's always sneaking out of the office for weird oxygen facials. Tell me you're not enjoying this too, Beanie."

"It's all right." I pause. "OK, it's pretty good. In fact, I think I could get used to it."

And that's where Claire finds us half an hour later. She's wearing a black ballet leotard and white footless tights, and her hair is slicked back into a high bun. She's getting a few funny looks from the naked ladies, but she seems oblivious.

"Hey, girls. I've been looking all over for you. Never thought I'd catch you in *here* with the nudie babushkas. Quite something, aren't they?" She nods at a group of voluptuous older ladies who are gathered at the far end of the pool, chatting away, all completely naked.

"Your photographer's at the swimming pool," Claire continues. "He's a little overwhelmed, I think. The other dancers can be a bit intimidating sometimes. Scary, in fact." She nibbles at the edge of a nail.

Remembering what she said about her nails in her diary entry, I look at her hands, and sure enough, they're bitten to the quick, and the skin around them is red and raw.

"Sorry about all this photo-shoot business," Clover says. "I'm sure you have better things to do, but I hope the interview will help ticket sales back in Dublin. And you look perfect, by the way. The image of a successful ballerina. And check out those arms. I bet you could lift an elephant with those babies."

Claire shrugs. "I guess they are pretty big for a girl, but most dancers have them. Ballet's a very demanding discipline. I don't think people realize how fit we have to be and how hard we have to train." She seems uneasy talking about herself and quickly changes the subject. "Anyway, how was your flight? And what's your hotel like?"

As we walk toward the pool, Clover tells Claire all about her luggage fiasco. I follow a little behind them, trying to keep my gaze straight ahead. I get enough nakedness at home. Alex loves stripping and running around the house in the nude. But toddler flesh isn't as scary as Budapest babushka flesh.

Claire, with her toned back and long, elegant neck, looks every inch the ballerina. She even moves like a dancer; each step is graceful, like she's flowing rather than walking. But there's also a deep sadness in her somehow that never seems to go away, even when she smiles.

Claire is right about Roland. He's totally out of his depth and completely in awe of the dancers. He seems too scared to tell them how to pose or to give them any direction at all. Luckily, Clover knows precisely what type of shots Saffy is after, and Roland seems happy to be bossed around. My nutty aunt stands there, her towel tucked around her body, telling him exactly what he's doing wrong. I did suggest she get changed first, but she pooh-poohed the idea. "No point. I'm so going back to that dreamy-steamy hot tub as soon as this is wrapped up. It's heaven on a biscuit."

She is snapping her fingers at the photographer now. "Roland, mush, we don't have all day. They're dancers, not models. Let them move and use their bodies. We're looking for action, power. Think gladiators, not beauty queens."

"Warriors, yes?" he asks.

"Exactly. Powerful, strong, but edgy, like panthers. Claire, can you do a warrior-type pose, please? Pretend Roland is the enemy and you want to kill him. Lean forward and glare at the camera. Amazing, Claire, that's perfect!"

Clover is right: if looks could kill, Roland would be stone dead.

"Now flex the muscles in your arms and neck, Claire. Brilliant!" Clover continues. "Right, girls, can you stand behind Claire and try some similar expressions? Think fierce thoughts, get it? And put some movement into the poses. Excellent!"

Roland quickly fires off a barrage of shots, capturing Claire and some of the other dancers as they glare at the camera while twisting and spinning their amazingly toned bodies around the pillars of the baths and around one another.

All the way through the photo shoot, Claire's eyes burn, like she really does want to kill someone. I begin to wonder if the enemy Claire is imagining as she stares angrily at Roland is in fact Zsuzsanna.

After the shoot, we soak in the baths for another hour, until our fingertips really do look like prunes, and then hole up in a café that Claire recommended that has wifi so that Clover can check her e-mail.

After licking the last crumbs of Domino chocolate cake off her fingers (another of Claire's suggestions and superdelicious), Clover passes me her laptop.

"Here, Beanie, sing for your supper. You work on this agony-aunt letter while I start on my piece for Saffy. It's time to fly solo, little swallow."

"Are you sure?" I ask her.

"Sure as eggs is eggs. Get cracking. Cracking? Get it — eggs? God, I *crack* myself up sometimes."

Dear Clover and Amy,

I'm thirteen and I'm really into swimming. I've recently joined a swim club, which means getting up at five and training from six until seven thirty four mornings a week. It's a killer, but it's worth it. My times have improved so much, and I have a real chance of winning nationals this year.

But there's a slight hitch. At the pool I used to go to, there were individual cubicles to change in, but at the new place, there's only one changing area and everyone strips together. I HATE it! I get so embarrassed. I wear my suit to the pool, but I can't wear my wet suit home! I get so embarrassed when I'm getting changed that I can feel my cheeks go scarlet. I get all clumsy. Plus, it takes me ages to dry off and put my clothes on, as I'm trying to keep everything covered up the whole time.

Some of the girls stand around chatting in their bras and knickers, or even worse, in the nude. I try not to look, but it's really hard. They all have boobs, and some of them have to shave under their arms and have hair you know where. I'm skinny with really wide shoulders and no boobs or hips, and I look more like a boy than a girl.

Sometimes I catch one of the girls staring at me, and it's so humiliating. I know they're thinking, "Shouldn't he be in the boys' changing room?" It makes it hard to concentrate in the pool, knowing I have to climb out and face the dreaded scramble into my clothes. And I'm concerned it will start affecting my times if I can't stop worrying about it. I've tried changing in the toilet cubicle, but there's only one and I was holding everyone up.

I know in the larger scheme of things that this is probably a very small dilemma, but if there's anything you can suggest that might help, I'd be very grateful. I love your problem pages in the *Goss*. You give such cool advice, and you're always so honest with people.

Bye,
Hannah in Dalkey

**I get started straightaway.**

Dear Hannah,

I know exactly how you feel! I hate changing in front of other people after field hockey. It's cringe-a-rama to the max. But I've had to get used to it. It's part of being on the team. One thing that has helped — and I know it probably sounds like a bit of a quick fix, but believe me, it works — is having nice underwear. I have a really fabarooney aunt and recently she bought me some *très* cool bras and knickers. If you don't have much to put in a bra — and I'm your sister there — try a padded one.

Now, you say you're tall and slim. Do you know how many girls would *kill* to be in your shoes? No wonder they're staring at you! You'd love boobs and hips? Well, I bet some of the more curvy girls would love a teeny waist and slim hips. And everyone worries about their body a bit, even grown-ups like my mum. I certainly do. It's normal. But remember, it's who you are on the inside that counts. I know that's easy to say, but it's the truth.

If swimming is your passion, and it sounds like

it is, don't let anything stand in the way of going for gold. Especially your own inner critic.

Here's my advice: Step one, go underwear shopping; and Step two, try telling yourself, "I love my body," every single day. One day you might just convince yourself!

And good luck at nationals, Hannah. I hope you smash it!

Yours,

Amy, also 13 xxx

I decided not to include Clover's name this time, as she's curves-and-boobs central. This one's especially to Hannah from me. I read over my answer, make a few tweaks, and then, satisfied, sit back in my seat.

Clover looks up from her notebook. "Finished, Bean Machine?"

"Yep. Will you read it over, Clover? In case I've made any mistakes."

"Sure thing, Beanie, old girl."

"Perfecto," she says after a few minutes. "Couldn't have done better myself. And you'll have super boobs one day, Beanie, never fear. I'm stacked and Sylvie's no slouch in the hubba-hubba department."

"Clover!" I blush a little, but she just laughs.

"You've signed it 'Yours, Amy.' No Clover this time? You giving little old *moi* the agony-aunt heave-ho?"

"Of course not. I just thought for this particular letter—"

"Don't worry, it's coola boola. I'm only teasing you." Then a serious expression takes the place of her smile. "But, you know, I will have to leave the *Goss* at some stage, Beanie, don't you? What with college and everything?"

My heart tightens in my chest. I can't imagine not working on the problem letters with Clover. It's part of who I am. Plus, it means I get to spend lots of time with my wacky aunt, not to mention travel to cool places like this. Being with Clover makes me feel more than I am—stronger, more confident. I *need* her.

She smiles at me. "Don't look so worried, Beanie. I'm not handing in my notice just yet. And fear not, I have a dastardly plan for the future that I shall reveal anon." She gives me a wink. "Now, you hungry? Right now, I could gnaw through a ballerina's leg."

"Clover, we've just demolished practically a whole chocolate cake each."

She just grins. "We're growing girls, Green Bean. We need serious femme fuel. More cake, darling?"

# ♥ Chapter 21

Today we're watching Claire in full ballerina mode, and we arrive at the Budapest Ballet's rehearsal rooms at ten past nine, as arranged. I press the intercom, while Clover whips off her pink boots and changes into her ballet flats. She's wearing two pairs of red tights (to keep her legs cozy) and my black-and-white Sonia Rykiel top over the red skater dress she wore on the plane, teamed with my silver belt. For someone with such limited outfit choices, she looks pretty fab.

A small white-haired woman meets us in the hallway. "Ladyshelf alert," Clover whispers in my ear.

"What?" I whisper back.

"Her boobs and her tummy meet in the middle. Look."

"Clover!" I hiss, but she's right, and it sets me off into fits of giggles.

The woman is peering at us both through half-moon glasses and tapping a lace-up shoe on the stone floor. Her eyes are dark and sharp, like a blackbird's. "The magazine girls?" she asks, her penciled-in eyebrows lifting. "You are writing about Claire Starr, yes?"

"That's right," Clover says, sticking out her hand politely. "Clover Wildgust and my assistant, Amy Green."

The woman ignores Clover's hand. "I am Madame Pongor, from the Ballet Academy. I was asked to look after you today, as my English is excellent. This way, and quickly. You are late, and Monsieur Elfman, the ballet master, does not take kindly to being interrupted."

We follow her down the corridor to a door at the end. Classical music is playing inside the room beyond. When it stops, Madame Pongor twists the door handle and opens the door, slowly and carefully.

The large, bright room is full of dancers, the girls in leotards and tights, the boys in T-shirts and tights or sweat shorts. A wiry older man with long silver hair tied back in a ponytail is standing at the top of the room. This must be Monsieur Elfman. He's wearing a black polo shirt and black trousers and is holding a long stick in his hand. He nods at us. "Enter," he says in heavily accented English. "Sit." He points his stick at a wooden bench that runs along one wall. "Thank you, Madame Pongor." He gives her a little bow, then turns his attention back to the dancers. "Journalists, necessary evil," he tells them.

I spot Claire at the back of the room. She is standing beside Péter and attacking one of her nails again. I catch her eye and she waves at me and mouths, "Hi."

Monsieur Elfman looks at us again. "Ballroom scene," he says simply. "Juliet dances . . . Ready, Juliet?"

Claire nods. "Yes."

"Places, please, everyone," Monsieur Elfman says. He bangs his stick on the floor. "Chop-chop."

The dancers move around the room, and suddenly they are no longer young girls and guys in practice clothes; they are lords and ladies at a posh Italian ball, all chins in the air and haughty looks. It's an amazing transformation. Clover takes out her notebook and scribbles down some notes for her article.

"Music." The ballet master taps his stick yet again, and the pianist starts to play.

Claire transforms in front of our eyes. She's Juliet

185 ♥

now, not Claire Starr. As the music plays, she starts dancing, sweeping across the room on her tippy-toes, raising her legs to impossible heights, jumping, spinning. She makes it look so easy. When Péter walks toward her as Romeo, there's such instant chemistry that the room practically crackles.

"Tender, Romeo," says Monsieur Elfman. "You are bewitched, mesmerized. At the moment, you look like a bull in heat."

Péter softens his expression and relaxes his neck and shoulders, which makes him look completely different. It's amazing to watch.

"Good, Romeo, that's perfect," Monsieur Elfman says. "Now Romeo is leaving the ballroom, Juliet. Follow him with your eyes."

The ballet master watches Claire carefully for a few minutes, then taps his stick again and gives a dramatic sigh. "Stop! Claire, Claire, Claire, you must be vulnerable, yes, confused? Dig deeper. You need to show more emotion. Let the audience feel how you feel. You are fifteen and about to be married off to an older man whom you do not love. So you are sad, yes? Then *bang*! Romeo enters your life. You are intrigued by this boy. He is young and handsome and he gives you hope. Your expression changes. You are now flirty, playful. I should not have to explain this to you again. . . . Zsuzsanna, show Claire what I am talking about, please. Claire, watch carefully."

Claire looks upset and embarrassed. "Can I try again?" she asks the ballet master. "I think I understand now."

"I thought she was great," Clover whispers to me.

I nod silently. I can't believe Monsieur Elfman is picking on Claire in front of us. I wonder what he's like when he doesn't have an audience.

"The whole scene from the top," Monsieur Elfman says, ignoring Claire's question. "With Zsuzsanna as Juliet this time."

Claire moves to the side of the room and watches as the dancers take their places once more. A blond girl with icy-blue eyes steps confidently into the center of the room to take Claire's place. So this is Zsuzsanna, Claire's tormentor.

"Claire!" the ballet master barks at her. "Pay attention."

Claire has been staring down at the floor, but now she looks up, her cheeks flaming, and murmurs, "Sorry."

Clover and I exchange a look.

"Yikes," Clover says softly. "Poor Claire. I'd love to say something to that man."

"Don't, Clover. It will only make things worse."

Zsuzsanna dances the role perfectly. Her face is all sad at the start of the scene, and then, when Romeo enters the ballroom, she beams and bats her eyelashes at him. It isn't subtle, but Monsieur Elfman seems satisfied. "Good, Zsuzsanna. You understand, Claire?"

Claire nods silently. One of her cheeks is distorted and it looks like she's biting down on it, hard. Zsuzsanna is smiling at her smugly, and Claire stares down at the floor again.

After the rehearsal, there's a lingering smell of exertion and sweat in the air as the dancers collect their things and layer on extra clothes. A lot of them are putting their hoods up or wrapping towels over their heads and around their shoulders to keep them from getting cold, which makes them look very odd. Roland joins us to take some action shots of Claire and Péter dancing together in their rehearsal gear. As he talks to Clover about the shoot, I stand at the side of the room with Claire, waiting for the other dancers to leave. Péter is chatting to Monsieur Elfman.

"You OK?" I ask Claire in a low voice. "I can't believe that elf creature picked on you like that."

"No, he was right," Claire says. "I don't seem to be able to tap into how Juliet is feeling in the ballroom scene. Yes, I could pull faces like Zsuzsanna, but I want the emotion to be real, not put on."

"Did you say something about me?" Zsuzsanna asks, suddenly appearing in front of Claire.

Claire shakes her head, looking panicked. "No, of course not."

"Who is in charge here?" Zsuzsanna asks me, practically pushing Claire out of the way and glaring at me with her steely eyes.

"Clover," I call. "Clover!"

Clover spins around. "What's up, Beanie?"

Before I get the chance to say anything, Zsuzsanna cuts in. "You should take photograph of real Hungarian dancer like me. You saw me dance. I am much better than Claire Starr. She is dancing Juliet in Dublin only because she is Irish. If we were dancing in Hungary, I would be Juliet, not her."

"Thanks for the offer," Clover tells her politely. "But we need only Claire and Péter today, not the chorus."

Zsuzsanna's eyes flash. "I am a senior soloist. How dare you!"

"I am so sorry for insulting you," Clover says, not sounding sorry at all. "I'm afraid I'm really busy, so I can't stop to talk, but it was nice meeting you."

Zsuzsanna's nostrils flare a little. "My name is Zsuzsanna Hommer. Madame Pongor has my number." (Man, she's stubborn.) "You ring me for interview later, yes? I very famous in Hungary. I have been in many Hungarian magazines."

"Bully for you," Clover says. She presses her foot against mine. Like me, Clover knows exactly what this girl has been up to, and how cruel she's been to Claire.

At that moment, one of the other dancers calls to Zsuzsanna, and she wafts her hand at her. "OK, I coming. You will ring, yes?"

"*Absolument.*" Clover trills her fingers at Zsuzsanna. "Bye-bye now. And *póg mo thóin.*"

Zsuzsanna's eyes narrow. "What did you just say?"

"It means 'break a leg' or '*merde*' in Irish," I explain quickly. It most certainly does not. It means "kiss my bum," which is pretty rude!

Zsuzsanna nods and *finally*, walks away.

"That bun-head is scary," Clover says, shaking her head.

"Tell me about it," Claire says, sounding defeated. "And I have to deal with her every single day."

"She's not as good as you are, Claire," I say desperately. "You know that, right?"

Claire just shrugs.

"Is anything wrong, Claire?" Clover asks. "If you want to talk . . ."

Claire starts picking at the side of a fingernail. "No, I'm fine, honest. I'm just nervous about dancing Juliet, that's all."

Péter appears beside us then. "Sorry about that. I needed to talk to Monsieur. So, ready for our photos, Claire?"

"I guess so," she says, still sounding a bit down. "I hope I don't make a mess of them."

Clover squeezes Claire's shoulder. "You'll be great," she tells her. "I've asked Roland to shoot you in all your hot and sweaty glory. I want our readers to be able to see your passion and your dedication. So lots of action shots. Take it away, Romeo and Juliet."

But Claire surprises us. Away from the critical eyes of Monsieur Elfman and Zsuzsanna, she's a different dancer. Like a butterfly who's just discovered her wings, she flies through the air, jumping fearlessly into Péter's arms with some strong, confident gazelle-like leaps. Roland catches it all on film.

"Bravo!" Clover cries. "Fantastic! Keep it up, guys, we're nearly there."

After a few more shots, Clover stops Roland and they look at some of the photographs together. Then Clover claps her hands. "We have exactly what we need. OK, guys, that's a wrap!"

Claire's face is shiny. She smells of fresh sweat,

and her chest is still pumping from all the exertion. "I have duet practice with Péter now," she says a little breathlessly, "but I'm around later this afternoon if you'd like to hook up. We could meet outside the academy at four, if that suits. Grab a coffee or something. I know you have some more questions for me, Clover."

"Coola boola, babes," Clover says. Then she shakes her head and smiles. "And how amazingly awesome were you? You can dance, girl!"

"Isn't she incredible?" Péter says, his chest still heaving from all the lifts. "You'll make a stunning Juliet, Claire."

Claire winces. "I just wish Monsieur Elfman agreed with you both. Now, we'd better not keep Madame Irina waiting. See you guys later."

And with that, we're left alone in the empty rehearsal room for a few seconds, until Madame Pongor, the woman from earlier, bustles in.

"You get what you needed?" she asks.

"Yes, thanks," Clover says. "Seeing Claire rehearse was a real privilege. Thanks for letting us watch. We really appreciate it. She's such a fantastic dancer. I had no idea."

Madame Pongor actually smiles, making her look less like a witch and more like a kind old granny. "She is good, yes. Beautiful fluid movements, wonderful expressive face. Such potential. She just needs more confidence onstage, more spark. In fact, she reminds me of Olga Varga in her early days. You hear of Olga, yes? Prima ballerina with this company many, many years ago. One of the best dancers the academy has ever produced."

"Of course we know her. Claire worships her," I say. "She has a picture of Olga on her bedroom wall back in Dublin."

"Olga would like that," Madame Pongor says. "She is Irish too, you know."

"Are you sure she's Irish?" Clover asks. "The name doesn't exactly sound Irish."

Madame Pongor laughs. "It's her stage name. Her real name is Ethel Murphy-O'Connor."

Clover's eyes open wide, and I can almost hear the cogs in her brain turning. A famous *Hungarian* prima ballerina who is actually *Irish*. That's one big scoop, all right!

And then something occurs to me. "Madame, does Claire know that Olga — Ethel, I mean — is Irish?"

Madame Pongor shrugs. "Ethel came to the academy as a young woman, like Claire. No one spoke much English back then, so she had to learn

Hungarian very quickly. When she joined the ballet company, she changed her name to Olga Varga. I think most people assumed she was from Budapest, and she never contradicted them."

"Does she still dance?" I ask.

"No, she retired in her late thirties, married a Hungarian art dealer, and had a son. But she still lives in Budapest."

"You don't happen to know where Ethel lives, do you?" Clover asks. "I'd love to interview her for my article."

Madame Pongor pauses, then says, "Ethel was never fond of the spotlight. She has a quiet life now. She does not go out so often."

"I understand," Clover says, looking disappointed.

"But do you think she'd talk to Claire?" I ask. "About what it was like when she was starting out, being Irish in a Hungarian ballet school, not speaking the language and everything. Claire's really nervous about dancing Juliet, and I think it might help."

Madame Pongor looks at me, considering this. Eventually she says, "Ethel is a kind lady, and she always supported younger dancers in the company. Yes, I think she would do this. And she might even give an interview to an Irish journalist, you never know. I will ring and ask her if you can visit."

Clover and I exchange an excited look.

"We're in like Flynn," Clover whispers to me. "Nice work, Batgirl."

# ♥ Chapter 22

It took us a few minutes to persuade Claire to come with us to find Olga Varga, aka Ethel Murphy-O'Connor. At first she just didn't believe us. "Olga Varga can't be Irish," she said. "It doesn't make any sense. I know Olga still lives in Budapest, but Madame Pongor must have gotten it wrong. I've read dozens of articles and interviews with Olga, and she's never mentioned Ireland — not once."

I explained what Madame Pongor had said about Ethel learning Hungarian early on and then changing her name.

Claire shrugged. "I think it's highly unlikely, but hey, nothing to lose, right? It'll be an adventure if nothing else." But she still sounded thoroughly unconvinced.

We follow Madame Pongor's directions. She wrote them down for us and kindly drew a small map so that we wouldn't get lost. Ethel's apartment is only a short walk from the rehearsal rooms, but it's freezing outside, so we walk quickly, our feet crunching over the cleared but icy sidewalks, our breath lingering in the air. We stop outside (another) tall gray building with a wooden door.

"I think this is it," Clover says, checking Madame Pongor's notes again. "Yep. Number thirty-seven Múzeum Utca. Do you want to do the honors, Claire? Apartment seven."

"Sure." Claire presses the intercom for apartment seven and we all wait nervously, stamping our feet to keep them warm.

"*Igen?*" a voice says.

"Excuse me, I'm looking for Ethel Murphy-O'Connor," I say politely into the intercom. "Is she in?"

There's a brief pause. "Are you one of the Irish journalists whom Maria — sorry, Madame Pongor — rang me about?"

Clover and I exchange an excited look. The voice is 100 percent without a doubt Irish.

"Keep going," Clover whispers to me.

I take a deep breath. "Yes. My name is Amy Green.

I'm from a magazine in Dublin. I was hoping I could talk to you about—"

"Ach, I've thought carefully about giving you an interview, and I'm afraid your journey has been wasted. I value my privacy too much. I'm sure you understand."

"But you *are* Ethel Murphy-O'Connor?" I ask.

"Yes," she says. "But I'm sorry, I must go."

"Wait!" Claire practically yells into the intercom. "Please? I have to know. Are you really Olga Varga?"

"Yes, but that was a long time ago, a past life. Are you from the magazine too?"

Claire is almost hyperventilating with excitement. "No! I'm Claire Starr. I'm a dancer with the Budapest Ballet."

"I've heard all about you from Maria, Claire Starr," Ethel says. "And I've seen clips of you dancing on the Internet. I didn't realize you were all arriving together. I think you'd better come in. But no interview, understand? And no photographs. This is completely off the record."

Claire looks at me and Clover. We both nod firmly.

"No interview," Claire promises.

Clover puts her hands on Claire's shoulders and

says in a low voice, "Maybe it's better if you go alone, Claire. We can stay down here and wait for you."

"Clover's right," I add. "And good luck."

Claire looks petrified, so I squeeze her hand, which is shaking like a leaf. It is scary meeting one of your heroes, all right.

"Don't be daft. Come on up, the lot of you," Ethel says through the intercom, making us all jump. We hadn't realized that she was still listening. "It's brass monkeys out there. Third floor, second door on the right."

The door buzzes loudly. Claire pushes it open and we troop in quickly, glad to get out of the cold. The hallway is paneled in dark wood and smells of furniture polish. We step into the small, slightly murky lift, and Claire presses the button for the third floor. She's biting her lip and can't keep still, shifting her weight from one foot to the other. By the time we get outside Ethel's apartment, it's not just Claire's hands that are shaking. Her whole body is twitching, and she looks like she's about to pass out.

"You OK?" I whisper.

She nods. "It's just . . . do you think this woman really is Olga Varga? I still can't believe it."

Clover puts her hand up to knock, but before she

gets a chance, the door swings open. And standing in front of us is the most attractive older women I've ever seen. She's in her late fifties or early sixties, and she's wearing beautifully cut black trousers with a ribbon bow at her tiny waist, a white cashmere roll-neck sweater, and matte-black heels. There's a dramatic cherry-red velvet scarf wrapped around her long, elegant neck that matches her red lipstick, and her silver hair is coiled on top of her head in a fancy chignon. Her huge navy-blue eyes sweep over us with interest.

Claire is staring at her as if she's seen a ghost. "Olga Varga," she says and gasps. "It's really you."

"Why, yes, my dear," the woman says. "But please call me Ethel. And do come in."

We step into the living room of her apartment. It's stunning: large and airy, and the white walls are covered in huge, bright abstract paintings that I can't stop gazing at. One of them looks just like a Rothko with its three huge squares of color in red, yellow, and orange. But it can't be an original, 'cause they're worth millions. There's a bronze sculpture of a dancer on a wooden plinth in front of one of the three dramatic floor-to-ceiling windows. A huge vase of stargazer lilies stands on the floor in front of another window, making the room smell deliciously sweet. It's like something out of an interiors magazine.

"Wowzers!" Clover says with a whistle. "Beautiful apartment, Ethel. You have fab taste. I'm Clover Wildgust, by the way, and this is Amy Green. And you know Claire already."

"I do, and thank you for the compliment," Ethel says. "Now, do give me your coats, or else you'll boil in here." She holds out her arms and we peel off our layers and hand them to her. She puts them over the back of a chrome-and-white-leather armchair. Every movement she makes is graceful, like a swan's.

"Take a seat," she says, waving at the matching white-leather sofa. "Anyone like a tea or coffee?"

"Oh, no, thanks, we're fine," Claire says quickly. I think she's afraid that she's dreaming, and that if Ethel leaves the room, the spell will be broken.

"But thanks for the offer," Clover adds.

All three of us sit on the enormous sofa. Ethel pulls an armchair around a little until it faces us and sits too, her back poker straight. Gran would have swooned at her posture. She was always telling me to stop slouching.

"So you're the Irish Ballerina," Ethel says, smiling warmly at Claire and leaning forward a little. "I've heard a lot of good things about you."

"Thanks," Claire says, her cheeks turning red. "And these are my friends from Ireland. They're over to do a feature on me for an Irish magazine." Claire makes a face. "So embarrassing."

Ethel throws her head back and gives a surprisingly deep and fruity laugh. "Awful, isn't it? I hated it too, believe me. And all the stupid posing for photographs. 'Look strong but vulnerable, Olga.' 'Let's dress you up as a black cat, Olga.' 'Pretend you're a warrior, Olga.' Such nonsense. All I wanted to do was dance."

Warrior? That sounds familiar. Smiling to myself, I press my foot against Clover's, and she gives me a tiny smile back.

"Yes, exactly," Claire says. "When I was younger, I thought I'd love all the publicity and being in the spotlight, but actually I'm finding it really difficult at the moment. And the other girls hate the fact that I'm getting all the attention. Especially when they don't believe I'm good enough for the part in the first place. . . ." She trails off and starts scratching at the side of her nail.

Ethel looks at Claire, her eyes kind. "Yes. It's very hard. But you must try to filter all that noise out of your mind and focus on the dancing. If you listen to what other people say, you will drive yourself crazy.

It sounds to me like some of the Hungarian girls are making your life difficult. Is that the case, my dear?"

Claire says nothing and just stares down at her hands. There's a large drop of blood at the side of one of her fingers. She must have scratched the skin so hard that she made herself bleed. She takes out a tissue and wraps it around the finger.

"Claire?" Ethel says gently. "Can I get you a bandage?"

Claire blushes furiously. "I'm sorry . . . it's nothing." She looks like she's about to cry.

Ethel says nothing for a moment and just sits there, watching Claire carefully. Then she says, "Would you like to hear how I became Olga Varga, girls?"

"Yes, please," Clover says, sitting up. She drags her bag onto her knee and whips out her notebook.

"Clover!" I hiss.

"Sorry, sorry," she tells Ethel, putting the notebook back. "Force of habit. This is strictly off the record, don't worry."

Ethel looks at Clover. "I imagine you'd like to mention the visit when you are writing about Claire. To put her journey in context, perhaps. But I live a quiet life now. I work in the office at my husband's gallery, and I look after my grandchildren. I'm sure you'd write a lovely piece, but I don't want other journalists looking for me. I hope you understand, my dear."

"Of course," Clover says. "It's just unusual. In my experience, most people are dying to be interviewed."

Ethel smiles. "I can imagine. But I've always hated the limelight. And I managed to keep my private life just that when I was dancing by being careful about what I said. I'm loath for anyone to start digging up the past now."

"Don't worry, your secret's safe with us," Clover says. "I promise. So, please, do tell us your story."

Ethel settles back in her seat and cups her long hands in her lap. "I came to the academy as a young girl, just like you, Claire. My family was originally from Wexford, but we moved to London when I was eleven, and I started ballet lessons, as there weren't any Irish dancing classes locally and I loved to dance. When I was seventeen, my ballet teacher put me forward for auditions for the Budapest Ballet Company. I was on the young side, and my technique wasn't strong enough, so they asked me to attend the academy for a year, and after that, if I improved, they promised me a place.

"As you can imagine, my parents weren't exactly

thrilled. It was the early seventies and no one knew all that much about Eastern Europe back then. But I nagged and nagged and finally they gave in."

Claire gives a tiny laugh.

"Does that sound familiar?" Ethel asks her.

"Totally," Claire says. "My folks were dead set against it. But I managed to talk them around too. I can be pretty persuasive when I want to be."

"Good for you. So I joined the academy and I worked my heart out, getting up early to practice every morning and dancing late into the night. Most of the teachers had no English, so I asked Maria — Madame Pongor — to give me Hungarian lessons every day in exchange for English lessons, and those helped a lot."

"Madame Pongor, really?" Claire asks. "She's scary."

Ethel smiles. "She's a pussycat underneath that gruff front. And she's passionate about ballet. Eats, sleeps, and breathes it, even though she's never danced professionally herself. She's a good person to have on your side. We are great friends to this day.

"Anyway, a year later, when I was eighteen, the academy offered me a place in the company. At first it was very difficult. The ballet masters were tough, and the girls . . ." She winces and shakes her head. "They did not like a Westerner in their company, dancing with their boys, taking their roles, and some of them made my life hell. Picked on me, told lies about me behind my back, even physically hurt me by kicking me in class."

Claire holds her hands together in her lap and blinks several times as if she's trying not to cry.

"It was because I was a threat to them, you understand?" Ethel continues. "Because I was good. And because they knew I had the potential to be great. So I had two choices. I could let them beat me — I could go back to London with my tail between my legs — or I could prove myself. So I changed my name to Olga Varga to show everyone how serious I was about being in the company. Nowadays having a Western name is no disadvantage, but back then it marked me as different. Then I worked harder than any other dancer. I got up earlier, I went to bed later. I danced until my toes were bruised and bleeding and then I danced some more.

"I listened to the music, *really* listened. I read the stories behind the ballets: the history. When I danced a role, I *became* that person. I inhabited the character's body. I knew my technique wasn't as perfect as some other dancers', but I also knew that I had more heart than they did, more passion, more drive. Once the ballet masters started to realize how much I gave to every role, they gave me bigger and bigger parts, until finally I had danced all the lead roles — in *Swan Lake, Giselle,* and *Romeo and Juliet,* just like you will, Claire. For you, Juliet is just the start of a wonderful career."

"And the bullies?" Claire asks.

Ethel looks her in the eye. "Yes, that is the right word, 'bullies.' I proved how good I was, how determined, and eventually they backed off. They realized that I wasn't going anywhere, and gradually we began to respect each other."

Ethel leans forward and takes Claire's hand. "How badly do you want this, Claire? Are you willing to risk everything, to put your heart and soul, your very being, into dancing Juliet?"

"Yes," Claire says. "But the girls. They pick on me all the time. There's this one girl who pulls my hair and kicks me and says things behind my back, things I don't even understand." Tears start to fall down her cheeks and she wipes them away with her free hand. "I'm sorry."

"Don't be sorry. Have you told your friends about this?"

"I don't really have any friends over here, not anymore. My roommate, Lana, was too heavy, so she had to leave the academy."

"What about your family?"

Claire shakes her head.

Ethel looks concerned. "You must talk to someone about this, Claire, understand? And you're not alone. It happened to me too, remember? I got through it, and you can too. Other dancers lash out because they feel threatened. You have such potential, and they're jealous. But you must rise above it. You can't let them get to you. When they realize they cannot break you, they will back off. And if the kicking and the hair pulling don't stop, you tell the person responsible that you will report her. And if she pays no attention, you come and tell me. And together we will talk to Maria and the head of the company, OK? You cannot let this ruin your career, Claire. And as for the language barrier, you will learn. I will teach you Hungarian. Including all the best juicy swear words."

Claire stares at her. "Really? You'd do all that for me?"

"Yes. Ballet has been good to me. I'd like to give something back, and we Irish ballerinas have to stick together. Without Maria's support, I'm not sure I would have made it either. Besides, I miss talking about dancing. My husband and son don't have that much interest." Ethel's still holding Claire's hand and now she clasps it with her other hand and squeezes tight. "Claire, all this bullying has made you doubt yourself and your ability to dance Juliet, am I right?"

Claire nods silently, her eyes glittering with tears again.

"You must try to remember who you were before you started having these thoughts," Ethel says. "Find a way back to that excited, passionate teenager who has just been accepted into one of the best ballet academies in the world. Can you do that?"

"I don't know, but I'll give it my best shot. I want to dance, Ethel. I want it more than anything else in the world. I'll die if I can't dance. But it's just been so hard . . ."

Ethel nods. Now there are tears in her eyes too. She releases Claire's hand and sits back in her chair again. "I know, my dear. Believe me, I know better than anyone. So, let's exchange mobile numbers, and in the new year we can arrange your first Hungarian lesson, OK? And you can tell me all about dancing in front of the home crowd. It's something I never got to do, unfortunately. The Budapest Ballet Company made it to London, but never to Dublin. Until then, Claire Starr, Irish Ballerina *extraordinaire*, I want you to be the best Juliet you can be. Give it everything, understand?"

"I will," Claire promises. "And Ethel? You were

an amazing dancer, one of the greats. I watch your DVDs all the time. No one has ever come close to your Juliet."

Ethel lifts her chin and beams. "Thank you, my dear. I was rather fabulous, wasn't I? And you will be just as good one day, maybe even better. Have faith, Claire."

We walk Claire back to her digs, stamping footprints into the fresh snow, which is falling in big swirling flakes. Claire doesn't stop smiling once.

"Olga Varga," she keeps saying. "I can't believe we've just met Olga Varga—Ethel, I mean. And she's offered to give me Hungarian lessons! Was I dreaming? Did that really just happen?"

"Abso-doodle-lutely," Clover says. "And you heard the woman. She thinks you could be just as good as her one day."

"She was just being kind," Claire says.

"She didn't seem the 'just being kind' type," Clover says. "In fact, she reminded me a lot of a certain someone, a certain rather determined Irish Ballerina."

Claire laughs. "I should be so lucky. Olga Varga's a living legend. And I can't believe she was bullied too."

"It all sounds horrible, Claire," I say. "The kicking and everything. Are you all right?"

She sighs. "I will be. Ethel's right. I have to stand up to them. I can't throw everything away just because of one stupid jealous cow." She shakes herself. "But let's forget all that now. I could murder a hot chocolate. And then I'm going straight home to write down every single word of what just happened in my diary before I forget. It's been quite a day."

I almost stop in my tracks. Of course! I've been so stupid. The diary doesn't hold the solution to Claire's problem. It *is* the solution.

"How long have you been keeping a diary?" I ask her, trying to keep my voice light.

"Since I first arrived in Budapest, why?"

"You know what Ethel was saying about remembering who you used to be? Well, if you read your diary backward, it will do just that. It will take you back in time, day by day."

Claire stares at me, her eyes bright, and for a second I think the game's up. But then she just smiles. "You know something? That's a great idea, Amy. I'll read my diary. But not backward. I'll start with my first week in Budapest. Ethel is right. I was unbelievably excited. I wanted to dance so badly — to be the best prima ballerina the world has ever seen. As good as

Olga Varga, in fact. And I knew I had the talent to do it. I wouldn't have let anyone stand in my way, and certainly not an overacting pig of a dancer like that Zsuzsanna Hommer."

While Claire is standing at the counter of the coffee shop — she insisted on paying as our reward for the Olga Varga discovery — Clover is looking at me, a huge beam of a smile on her face.

"Why are you grinning at me like a lunatic?" I ask.

"You did good, Beanie. I know you still feel guilty about reading Claire's diary, but don't. It was the right thing to do."

"The end justifies the means?" I say.

"*Exactement*, Bean Machine. You can now delete the file and erase all trace of what you were up to. And, of course, your secret is safe with me."

As I smile back at her, I feel the guilt fall off my chest and spin in the air like a Hungarian snowflake.

♥ Chapter 23

"I can't believe we're back in boring old Dublin already," I moan, stepping onto the Aircoach at Dublin airport behind Clover. It's Sunday, early evening.

"I know, but I am looking forward to wearing my own clothes for a change. Kudos to your mum for tracking down my bag," Clover says. "Although I'm growing kind of fond of this Puffa jacket. It's Budapest blingtastic."

"It sure is —" I'm cut off by my mobile ringing.

"Amy, you're back," says the voice at the other end of the line. It's Dad. "Did you have a good time? How was Budapest?"

"It was fab," I tell him. "We soaked in the baths and ate loads of chocolate cake, and we even got to see

Claire dancing. So what's up with you, Poparooney? Any news?"

"Yes, actually, that's why I'm ringing. I thought you'd like to know that Gracie's first tooth has just come through. She now has a tiny tooth in the middle of her bottom jaw."

"Cute," I say. "Is she crying a lot? Evie always cries when she's teething."

"All the time," Dad says. "Last night Shelly had to get up —" He stops abruptly. "Hang on, I just heard the doorbell. Stay there. I'll be back in a second."

I hear voices and then a woman shrieking, "Yes, yes, yes!" What on earth is going on in Dad's house?

Finally he comes back on the line and says, "Amy, I have to go. I'll ring you back later."

"What's happening?"

"You won't believe this, but a man just arrived at the door, looking for Pauline. Then as soon as he saw her, he dropped to one knee and proposed, right on the doorstep. You probably heard her shrieking yes."

I gasp. It looks like my Send-Pauline-Packing plan may have worked. "No way!"

"I'd better go, Amy. Shelly looks like she's in shock. I guess it's not the ideal way to discover that your mum has a boyfriend."

OK, that *wasn't* part of the plan. "Ring me back as soon as you can, Dad."

"I will."

As soon as I click off the phone, Clover pounces. "What's going on, Beanie?" she demands.

"I think I'd better start at the beginning. You know how much Dad loves living with Pauline . . ."

Clover snorts and rolls her eyes. "Not!"

"Exactly. Well, I decided I'd try to help him get rid of her. And anyway, Pauline's miserable over here. She misses the sun and Dean, her boyfriend in Portugal. So I sent Dean a message on Facebook, saying how much I, well, *Pauline,* missed him. I found out her e-mail address and password when I was over at Dad's place one evening."

"And?" Clover says impatiently, her eyes wide.

"Dean sent her a lovely message back and a poem he'd written for her called 'My Achy-Breaky Heart Belongs to Pauline.' I waited for a few days to see if she'd reply, but she didn't. She mustn't have spotted the message and I didn't want him to think she'd changed her mind or anything . . ."

The edges of Clover's mouth twitch. She clutches my arm. "Please put me out of my misery. Tell me you sent him a poem back, something really smoochy."

My cheeks flare guiltily.

Clover hoots with laughter. "Beanie, you so did! Coola boola. What was it, Shakespeare?" Her eyes are twinkling.

How did she guess? "Yes. I sent him one of Shakespeare's sonnets about 'the marriage of true minds,' and a poem by a man called Robert Burns about love being like 'a red, red rose.'"

"Ha! Good woman. And don't tell me, Dean is at your dad's house now, looking for Pauline."

"He's gone one better! He just proposed to her, right on the doorstep." My mobile rings again. "Hang on. It's Dad again."

"Amy, are you there?" Dad sounds in a bit of a state.

"What's wrong?" I ask. "Has Pauline decided to stay in Ireland?"

"No, she's going back to Portugal with Dean. He's already booked them both on a flight this evening. He says he has to get back right away to keep an eye on his pub. No, it's Shelly."

"Is she upset about Dean?"

"No, in fact she's excited for her mum about that. She's a bit shocked, of course, but she says she's thrilled to see her mum so happy. It was when she realized that Pauline was leaving immediately that she got upset. I think she blames me. She says if I'd made Pauline feel more welcome, she might stay a bit longer and help with Gracie. Shelly says she can't cope without her mum because I'm so hopeless at baby stuff and I'm always at work and she's exhausted from doing everything by herself. I've tried to explain that maybe I'd be more inclined to come home early if Pauline wasn't around all the time, but she just stormed off. She's even talking about going to live in Portugal with Pauline and taking Gracie with her. And I think she's serious."

Yikes, I hadn't anticipated that!

"And now Shelly's shut herself in our bedroom," Dad goes on, "and she won't talk to me. From the noise inside, I think she's packing. What am I going to do, Amy? I'll die without Shelly and Gracie. They're my life." I've never heard him so upset.

My stomach sinks into my Converses and I start to feel a little faint. What have I done? I was trying to get rid of Pauline, not Shelly.

"Dad, we're just going into the tunnel," I say, trying not to sound as panicked as I feel. "Can you hear me? . . . . No signal . . . Ring you back." And then I cut him off.

Clover is staring at me. "Tunnel, Beanie? What tunnel? What's going on now? You look like you've seen a banshee."

"I'm in troublesville, Clover. Deep, deep *merde*. Shelly's talking about moving to Portugal with Pauline and taking Gracie with her!"

"What! She can't do that. Dublin is Gracie's home. And Shelly's crazy about Art. Why would she do that?"

"I don't know. But I have to do something, Clover. I have to help Dad. He can't lose Shelly and Gracie, he just can't." My heart is hammering in my chest.

Clover says nothing for a few minutes. Then she pats my hand. "We're not going to let that happen, Beanie. Don't you worry, we'll think of something."

Dad is so relieved to see us on the doorstep, he nearly weeps. "Please tell me you've come to talk Shelly around," he says in a low voice. His face is gray, and I've never seen him look so worried.

Clover nods. "Yes. If we can."

"Thank God. If I lose my girls, I don't know what I'll do. Please do everything you can to make Shelly understand, OK? If she'll only talk to me . . ."

And for the first time ever, Clover gives him a hug. "We'll do our best, Art. But if we manage to get Shelly to speak to you, you have to promise to be a better dad to both Amy and Gracie."

"And Shelly's right. You do have to help with Gracie more, Dad," I add. "Where is Gracie, anyway? Is she OK?"

"She's fine," Dad says. "Dean's giving her a bottle. He's very good with babies, despite all the tattoos. Pauline's upstairs packing."

Clover smiles gently. "I can't wait to meet this Dean dude, but first Shelly. We'll do what we can, Art, OK? Promise."

Dad nods, his face still ashen.

I follow Clover up the stairs. Clover knocks on Dad and Shelly's bedroom door, and we both listen carefully. Nothing. She tries again. "It's Clover and Amy, Shelly," she says. "Can we come in?"

Silence.

"Please?" I say. "It's important."

The door opens a crack, and Shelly's blotchy face appears. "I know your dad sent you, Amy, and you can tell him, nice try but it's too late," she says, her voice cracked and breathy from crying. "My mind's made up. I can't look after Gracie on my own. I'm scared I'll do something wrong. I had no idea babies were so difficult. And Art's no use. If Mum leaves, I'll have no one to ask about rashes and coughs and teething and stuff. I can't do it alone, so I'm going to stay with Mum in Portugal until . . . until . . ." She starts crying. "I'm sorry, Amy. Really I am."

"Won't you just talk to Dad?" I beg.

"No. I have to go now." And the door shuts.

Clover and I look at each other. "What now?" I ask.

"There's only one person who is going to change Shelly's mind," she says in a low voice. "And that's Pauline. We have no other option."

I wince. "I wish it wasn't true, Clover, but you're right. Let's do it now before we chicken out."

Clover crosses herself and starts walking up the small flight of stairs toward Pauline's room. This time when Clover knocks, the door swings open immediately.

"Yes?" Pauline looks at us suspiciously.

"Can we talk to you, Pauline?" Clover says. "In private."

"About what?"

"Well, we want to congratulate you on your engagement, don't we, Amy?" Clover looks at me pointedly.

"Oh, yes, of course," I say. "Congratulations, Pauline. I hope you and Dean will be very happy together."

Pauline's eyes soften a little. "It is rather wonderful. Look!" She holds up her ring finger proudly. A massive diamond twinkles in the light.

"And you must be excited about going back to Portugal," Clover continues.

"Yes," Pauline says. "I can't wait. Dublin can be dreadfully wet and gray. I miss the sun so much."

"And I believe Shelly is considering joining you," Clover says carefully. "With Gracie. Do you really think that's such a good idea?"

Pauline shrugs. "If it's what my daughter wants, I can't stop her. Art's hardly much help, and she does need backup with Grace."

"He wants to help more," I say. "He's just not a baby person. Mum said he was exactly the same when I was little. As Gracie gets older, he'll get better."

Pauline snorts. "Do you honestly expect me to believe that? Art Green is selfish to the core. He's always working late or playing golf."

"Because he wants to get out of the house," I say with force. "He hates coming home because you're here."

Pauline gasps. "You can't talk to me like that. And that's not true."

"It is true," I say. "You're always picking holes in him in front of Shelly. He's been working late to avoid you. And they can't do stuff together like they used to 'cause you're always hanging around."

"I never meant to get in the way." Pauline sniffs. "But it's too late now. Shelly's made her decision, and that's that."

"You can't let this happen," I say. "Pauline, please listen to me. It's not right. Gracie deserves a full-time dad, and he really does love her. Gracie and Shelly are his life — he said that himself. OK, so he's not a baby person, but when Gracie is older, he'll be brilliant. From when I was about four until, well, until he left, he used to take me to the zoo or swimming or to the movies every Saturday afternoon. 'Amy-and-Daddy time,' we used to call it. We had so much fun together. And I still love him, even though I don't see him all that much. And what about Gracie, doesn't she count? It feels like I'm the only one sticking up for what she needs. And she needs her mum and her dad."

"Amy's right," Clover says. "Gracie needs both her parents. And Shelly is crazy about Art, you know she is. Leaving him will break her heart. And I've never seen Art so distraught about anything before. I think he genuinely loves Shelly. You have to do something, Pauline. Shelly will listen to you. Please?"

Pauline is quiet for a few moments, just standing there, staring down at her engagement ring and twisting it around and around on her finger. "Shelly was mad about her dad," she says finally. "He was a lovely man. Really lovely. He died when Shelly was eight. Heart attack. Dreadfully sad. I think she still misses him. Amy, your father is lucky to have you. I'm sorry if I've given you a hard time. But you don't make it easy to like you. You can be quite rude, you know. Quite the little madam."

I'm dying to say something back to this, but I bite my tongue.

"But it's obvious that you love your dad and your little half sister," Pauline continues.

"Sister!" I say.

"Sorry, sister. I'll talk to Shelly, but I'm not promising anything. And in exchange you have to do something for me, both of you. My Shelly can be a bit of a worrywart sometimes and a bit ditzy. If she decides to stay in Dublin, I'd like you to keep an eye on her for me. Will you do that?"

Clover looks at me and I nod.

"Of course," I say. "Tell Shelly to ring me if she's worried about Gracie. I'm good with babies. And she can always ask Dave for advice too. Dave's a nurse — remember? You met him at Gracie's christening — and I'm sure he'd be happy to help. I can give Shelly his mobile number."

"That's a brilliant idea, Beanie," Clover says. "You have such smarts sometimes."

"That would be reassuring for Shelly, I'm sure," Pauline says, and she actually smiles at me, a proper smile that makes her eyes twinkle.

When we go back downstairs, leaving Pauline to try to talk Shelly around, Dad is sitting at the kitchen table, Gracie cradled in his lap. I realize with a start that it's the first time I've seen him holding Gracie on his knee.

"Well?" he says as soon as we walk in.

"Pauline's talking to Shelly," I say. "Now we just have to wait. Where's Dean?"

"Taking a phone call in the sitting room." Dad strokes Gracie's soft baby hair. "Oh, Gracie, if your mum gives me a second chance, I'm going to be the best dad ever, I swear."

Ten minutes later, Pauline walks into the kitchen and we all look at her hopefully.

"Shelly says she'll stay as long as you help out more, Art," she says to Dad. "A lot more. And I've told her that I'll stay in Dublin for another two weeks and help her to find a part-time nanny so that she gets a break from Gracie when you're at work. And she'd love Dave's mobile number, if that's OK, Amy. She said that would really put her mind at rest."

"Dave?" Dad says, looking a little surprised.

"If Gracie is sick and Shelly's worried, she can ring him for advice," I explain.

Dad smiles at me. "Amy, you're one smart cookie. And Pauline, I, er, well, I'm, uh . . ."

"I think the word is 'thanks,' Dad," I say.

Dad looks sheepish. "I was actually going to say I'm sorry. I know we've had our differences, Pauline, but I hope we can put them all behind us now and be one big happy family."

Pauline doesn't look convinced. "If you mess up or upset my daughter in any way, Art Green, I'll be on the next flight back from Portugal. Understand?"

Dad gulps. "Yes, Pauline."

A tall, burly man with a mahogany tan walks into the room. It's Dean. I recognize him from the Facebook photos. His tattoos, swirling Celtic patterns like black snakes on both lower arms, are even more impressive in real life. He's completely bald, with a big beer belly stretching against his Manchester United top — not at all the kind of guy I would have pictured Pauline going for, but it just goes to show, wrinklies are very odd, indeed. As soon as she spots him, Pauline's eyes light up.

"Dean, I'd like you to meet Amy and Clover," she says, still beaming at him. "Amy is Art's eldest daughter and Grace's sister. Clover is Amy's aunt."

"Pleased to meet you both." Dean grins and shakes our hands warmly, and, boy, does he have a firm handshake!

Gracie starts to fuss. Her cheeks have gone bright red and she's dribbling a lot. Dad looks a little nervous. "Will you hold her, Amy? I think there's something wrong with her."

"It's just her teeth, Dad, remember? Mum keeps special soothers in the fridge for Evie to chew on. You could buy some at the pharmacy."

"OK, I'll do that. I'll just go up and see Shelly first. Will one of you take Gracie for me?" He looks around the room.

"No, Dad," I say. "Take Gracie with you. It will show Shelly that you mean what you've promised about helping out with her more."

Dad nods. "Good idea. And I know it's silly, Amy, but I'm kind of nervous. What should I say to her?"

"Just tell her what you told me, about how much you love her and Gracie. And that you'll try to help more and stuff. You'll be fine."

His eyes well up. "Thank you, Amy. I don't deserve you."

Clover rolls her eyes. "Holy Moly, guys, it's all getting a bit *Oprah* in here. I, for one, am starving. I could murder a pepperoni pizza. Let's get takeout. Oh, and it's on you, Art. Hand over your credit card."

"It's the least you can do, Art," Pauline adds firmly. "Hand it over."

"Yes, ma'am," Dad jokes, clicking his heels together.

I look at Pauline, hoping that she won't take offense, but she just laughs. Clover and I dissolve into fits of giggles. And after the last few hours, boy, does it feel good to be laughing again!

# ♥ Chapter 24

On Wednesday evening, Mum calls up the stairs, "Amy, surprise visitor for you."

I think for a second. It can't be Mills, as she's still not talking to me, and it's unlikely that Seth would stop in at nine p.m., so it must be Clover. I bound down the stairs. Clover always cheers me up, no matter how rotten I'm feeling, and as I've had a lousy day at school, I could really do with a pick-me-up. But halfway down the stairs I see that it isn't Clover standing in the hall with Mum. It's Claire Starr!

"Hi, stranger," she calls up at me. "Long time no see — not." She gives a big, happy laugh.

"Claire! What are you doing here?" I ask as, to my surprise, she gives me a warm hug. Her hair smells of chocolate muffins. Her mum's obviously been baking in honor of her homecoming.

"Why don't you guys go into the sitting room?" Mum suggests. "That way you won't wake up the babies."

"Sorry, Sylvie, I know it's late to visit." Claire looks a bit embarrassed.

"Not at all," Mum reassures her. "You're always welcome here, Claire, honest. But if Alex hears you, he'll be down like a shot. He's one very nosy toddler."

"I get you," Claire says. "And I'd love to meet the kids at some stage."

"Anytime, Claire," Mum says. "But wear clothes you can wipe clean."

Claire laughs again, probably thinking Mum's joking, and Mum goes off into the kitchen.

"Your mum looks well," Claire says as we sit down on the sofa in the living room.

"I guess. When did you get here?"

"This afternoon. The rest of the company is flying in tomorrow, but I wanted to spend some time with Mum and Dad before the show kicks off and things start to get really hectic. I'm going to try to get back more often from now on too. I know I've been neglecting everyone in Dublin. Hanging out with you and Clover in Budapest was so much fun. It made me realize how much I've missed home. And thanks for hooking me up with Ethel. She rang me to say good luck with the show, and we chatted for ages. Olga Varga wished *me* luck—well, *merde*, actually. Imagine. I'm going to dance my socks off, for her and for myself. In fact, I'm dying to get on that stage and show everyone what I can do. I'm going to be the best Juliet the critics have ever seen."

I laugh. "And you're so modest too, Claire."

"Modesty's for losers," she says. "I'm going to *smash* it. Péter thinks so too. He's such a sweet guy. I've told him about Zsuzsanna and what has been going on. He wanted to kill her, of course, but he knows that getting angry is not the answer. So everything's good, Amy, thanks to you and Clover."

I grin to myself. Maybe reading back over her old diary entries helped, or maybe meeting Ethel and realizing that she wasn't alone—that even the great Olga Varga was bullied once—gave Claire the confidence boost she needed, or maybe she would have bounced back anyway. In the end, it doesn't really matter. All I care about is that the old Claire Starr is totally and absolutely back!

"Anyway, I know Mills still isn't speaking to you," she continues. "She can be pretty stubborn, that sister of mine. I figured I owe you one, so I had a word with her, told her not to throw away everything you guys have because of a silly fight. She told me what happened, about reading your diary."

I can feel myself blushing.

"I didn't mean any of it. Not really," I explain.

Claire smiles gently. "I know. I keep a diary too, remember? You never expect anyone else to read it, do you?"

"No," I murmur. Even though I've deleted Claire's diary from my memory stick and will take her secrets to the grave, I still feel guilty. I'll just have to live with it, I guess. And I'll never, *ever*, read anyone's diary again, that's for certain.

"When Mills realized what it was, she should have stopped reading immediately," Claire adds strongly. "It was wrong, and she sees that now. We had a bit of a chat about boys too. The problem is, that thing you wrote about her wanting to be a cheerleader just because of Bailey was the truth, and she doesn't want to admit it to herself, let alone to anyone else. I hope you guys *can* work things out. You're very lucky to have each other."

"Thanks," I say, a faint glimmer of hope starting to dance in my stomach. "For talking to Mills, I mean."

"No, thank you, Amy. I'm not sure I would have

made it this far without you and Clover. Meeting Ethel has changed my life. And she was right about Madame Pongor. She is a sweetheart under that gruff exterior."

"How are things with Zsuzsanna?" I ask.

"OK. I told her I'd report her if she didn't stop picking on me. She didn't like that one little bit, but she's just ignoring me now, which is a big improvement."

"Good for you."

"Thanks. I was proud of myself, all right." She pauses for a second and looks a little worried. "Amy, you won't say anything to Mills or my folks about the bullying, will you? It would only upset them, and it's under control now."

"Of course not. I'm good at keeping secrets." If only she knew how good!

On Thursday morning, I wait at the letter box for Mills. It's where we usually meet to travel to school together, and I'm hoping that Mills's mood has thawed. But she doesn't show up.

On Friday morning, I try again, but again, no joy. Mills must still be leaving early to avoid me. She's supposed to be coming to the ballet tonight with

Clover, Mum, and me. I've texted her loads of times to ask if she's still coming, but she hasn't replied. I guess I know what that means. She still hates me.

I trudge off toward the train station, feeling dark and alone. And then I sit in a train carriage, alone. I've waited so long for Mills that I've missed the train Seth and Bailey always get. I can't stop thinking about Mills and how much I miss her. I've tried not to think about it too much, as it's so upsetting, but today it's like a scab I just have to pick, pick, pick. For some reason, I want to make myself feel even worse. I remember all the fun we used to have, the sleepovers when we stayed up all night, laughing until our stomachs hurt, writing lists of the famous boys we'd like to marry, drawing our fantasy wedding dresses (that was Mills's idea!), making up our faces like Lady Gaga and dancing around the bedroom, singing into hairbrushes, or playing Just Dance on the Wii until our bodies ached. My eyes start to fill with tears, and I blink them away and take a few deep breaths to steady myself.

As I'm walking up the road toward Saint John's, I get a text from Seth: FORGOT TO TELL YOU. OFF TO HOSPITAL WITH POLLY TODAY. WON'T BE IN SCHOOL. SEE YOU ON SAT XXX SETH

My heart sinks into my scuffed school shoes.

Seth often goes to the hospital with Polly when she's having her regular tests done, but did it have to be today? Oh, this day is just getting better and better.

At break, I spot Mills pulling books out of her locker and walk toward her, my stomach tense. "Mills?"

She turns to look at me, and we stand there for a few long seconds, staring at each other. Her cheeks go a little pink, and I can feel mine heating up too.

"Are you still coming to the ballet with Mum and Clover and me tonight?" I ask her. "Dad got us all tickets, remember? It'll be fun." I smile at her hopefully.

"Fun?" She gives a very un-Mills-like snort and slams her locker door shut. "As if I'd want to be anywhere near you, Amy Green. Get a life. And you're in my way. Move!"

She pushes past me, her books clutched against her chest.

"Mills!" I walk after her.

"Stop following me, Amy. I don't want to talk to you — not now, not ever. Get it?"

"I'm sorry, OK? I'm really, really sorry. I miss you. Please —" My voice cracks, and tears start to spill down my cheeks. Mills doesn't stop walking.

"Oh, Mills!" I hear a voice behind me. It's

Annabelle. Nina and Sophie are with her. Annabelle's mouth is twisted into a nasty scowl. *"Mills, don't do this to me,"* she says in a high-pitched baby voice. *"I'm all alonio and I have no fwends. Boo-hoo-hoo."* She pretends to cry into her hands.

"You're completely heartless, Annabelle Hamilton," I say, my stomach churning with upset and anger. "You're nothing but a big bully."

"At least I have friends, Amy Green," she says, sneering.

"You don't. People hang out with you only 'cause they're scared of you. One day you'll realize that."

"Well, even Mills Starr doesn't want anything to do with you, and she's, like, a total loser. Which makes you an even bigger loser."

"Don't talk about Mills like that. She's amazing and smart and funny — and loyal. And speaking of loyalty, shouldn't you be sticking up for her? She is a fellow cheerleader."

Annabelle laughs and tosses her hair, sending a waft of disgustingly sweet perfume into the air. "We are, like, so not friends. We only tolerate her 'cause we, like, need her so we can ace the nationals. After that, she's so off the squad. She so doesn't fit in. She's, like, a complete square. You know something? You two deserve each other. You're as pathetic as each other. Now, it's been, like, awesome talking to you, but we have to split."

"What makes you think I want to talk to you anyway, Annabelle Hamilton?" I say. But she's right. I have no friends, so nobody hears me.

That evening, I'm standing in front of my mirror, staring at the girl in the black jeans and plain black T-shirt, the girl with the dead eyes and the slumped shoulders, when I spot something sparkly out of the corner of my eye. It's the snow globe I bought Mills in Budapest. I must have knocked against it as I walked past my desk, because the tiny glittering "snow" particles are swirling around the tiny dancer inside it, like she's caught in a blizzard.

I pick it up and hold it in my hands, running my finger over its smooth glass surface. I know Mills would have loved it. Swallowing back the lump in my throat, I sit down on my bed and stare into space. I guess it's time to face facts. I'm going to have to learn to live without Mills, my best friend in the whole entire world.

Clover bounds through the door while I'm sitting there thinking and says, "Ta-da! You likey?" She drops the dark-pink shopping bag she's holding onto the floor and spreads out her arms, like she's tap dancing. She's wearing a black dress with a soft velvet top and a full, ballerina skirt made of layers and layers of tulle. "It's my homage to *Swan Lake.*"

"I thought we were seeing *Romeo and Juliet.*"

"It's all ballet smallet. So? Do I look super-duper or what?"

"You look beautiful, Clover," I say, my voice coming out a little flat.

"You don't seem very excited about the show, Beanie. What's up, jelly tot?"

"Mills," I admit. "She's not coming tonight. I've lost her, Clover. I've lost my best friend."

Clover sits down beside me and puts her arm around my shoulders. "Have you tried talking to her, babes?"

"Yes. But she won't listen to me. It's no use. She doesn't want anything to do with me, ever again."

Clover spots the snow globe that is still nestled in my hands. "That was for her, wasn't it?" she asks gently.

I nod. "Claire even tried talking to her for me, but it still didn't work."

"Give her the globe anyway. As a kind of farewell gift. Write her a note to go with it, saying how sorry you are. It will make you feel better about things later on. It might even give you some closure, as the Americanos say. I'll ask your mum for a padded envelope and I'll drop it over there while you get dressed, hon, OK?"

"I am dressed."

Clover leans forward and picks the shopping bag up off the floor. "For you, babes. I thought you could do with a little pick-me-up."

I pull out a black-silk puff-sleeved dress with tiny ballerinas all over it in white. It's adorable.

"Thanks, Clover."

"You're welcome, Beanie. Now I have to help Sylvie with her makeup, so write that notearooney, chop-chop." She tosses her head back, scowls at me, and taps her foot on the floor.

"Yes, Monsieur Elfman."

"Got it in one, Beanie." She laughs and then trips out of the room. As soon as she's gone, I rip a page out of my notebook, grab a pen, and start to write.

Dear Mills,
I saw this snow globe in the Christmas market in Budapest, and I thought of you. We're off to see Claire tonight without you, and it feels all wrong. We should be watching your sister

together, squealing and getting completely overexcited, until Mum shushes us and we squeeze each other's hands and try to stop giggling.

I'll be thinking of you when Claire comes onstage. You must be so proud of her. I'm sure you'll be going to see her over the weekend with your mum and dad. You might be going every night, for all I know. It's quite something, having a star like Claire in the Starr family. I know she's going to be stellar. (Get it?)

Mills, I'm so sorry about what happened. I wake up every day feeling sick, knowing I have to spend another day without my best friend by my side. I'll never have another friend like you as long as I live. You're one in a million: smart, funny, loyal, sweet, kind . . . all the things that I'm not.

I miss you so much, Mills. I'll always have a special place for you in my heart, no matter what. I'll put your ballet ticket in the envelope — you're such a scrapbook fiend that you might like it for your new Claire Starr scrapbook, 'cause, boy, are you going to need one!

Love you forever,
Amy xxx

# ♥ Chapter 25

"Everything all right, Amy?" Mum asks. We're sitting in our red-velvet seats in the Bord Gáis Energy Theatre and I'm concentrating on the stage, trying to stop thinking about how much Mills would love this place. It's truly breathtaking, with its soaring ceilings, made up of geometrical layers of wood, and mesmerizing lights in the shape of stars.

"Great." I smile across at her, trying to forget about the empty aisle seat to my right. We are only six rows from the stage, at the end of the middle row, and we have an amazing view. Clover's sitting to my left, and she squeezes my hand.

"Here we go, Ballet Bean, Claire's big moment," she says. "I don't know about you, but my stomach's turning pirouettes for her."

"Mine too."

There's an excited *hum* as the last few people take their seats and the lights begin to slowly dim. Then I hear a voice from the aisle. "Excuse me, is this seat taken?"

I look up. And standing there, looking nervous, is Mills. *Mills!*

I shake my head, unable to say anything and not daring to think about what this means.

She sits down beside me. "Thanks for the snow globe," she says. "It's beautiful. And your note meant a lot. I heard you sticking up for me today too, telling Annabelle I was funny and smart. Thanks. And I hate to admit it, but you were right all along. I did join the All Saints only 'cause of Bailey. But I really *like* cheering, Ames, and I'm good at it! I want to keep doing it — if Annabelle doesn't drive me out, or murder me or something. The thing is I should never have read your diary in the first place." She shrugs. "So I guess we're back to normal. If that's OK with you?"

For a second, I can't say anything. I'm so relieved and happy that I'm speechless. Then I finally find my voice. "OK?" I squeal. "It's brilliant." I fling my arms around Mills and hug her tight, my heart soaring. "And I'll always stick up for you, Mills. Always!"

"Claire told me about Budapest," she says after our hug. "And how you and Clover tracked down Olga Varga and everything. She said talking to Olga about her dance worries made all the difference. Thanks to you, Claire's back to her old annoying, bossy, confident self."

I laugh. "But you wouldn't have her any other way."

"Correct!" She laughs too.

"Girls," Mum hisses. "Keep it down now. It's about to start. But I'm glad you could make it, Mills. Good to see you."

"Me too," Clover says, giving me a big I'm-really-happy-for-you smile.

As the orchestra starts to play, Mills and I both giggle and squirm in our seats like little kids, trying to contain our excitement, just as I predicted.

"I've really missed you, Ames," Mills whispers. "Best friends."

"Forever," I add.

She grins, takes my hand in hers and holds it firmly, her palm warm against mine. I hope she never lets it go.

# ♥ Epilogue

**ARTICLE IN THE *IRISH TIMES:* "A STARR IS BORN"**

Last night, at the Bord Gáis Energy Theatre, a new ballet star was born. Dubliner Claire Starr danced her way into the headlines with her remarkable performance of Juliet in Budapest Ballet's delightfully fresh and vibrant production of *Romeo and Juliet.*

Starr's technique was near perfect, and she danced with such energy and confidence that it was impossible not to be swept away by her beautifully tender and emotional portrayal of one of Shakespeare's famous star-crossed lovers.

The packed auditorium quite clearly adored her, reflected by the ten-minute standing ovation.

When Starr and her Romeo, the powerful young Hungarian dancer Péter Bako, embraced and kissed during the curtain call, three high-spirited teenagers in seats near the front started to chant, "Olé, olé, olé, olé, Claire Starr, Claire Starr."

It's not hard to see why Starr inspires such devoted outbursts. Her dancing is world class, and this reviewer, for one, can't wait to see what she does next. Watch this space . . .

# Acknowledgments

This book would not have been possible without a LOT of people's help (my very own corps de ballet!). First up my light-footed family: Mum, Dad, Kate, Emma, and Richard. I love you all to bits. I wouldn't be able to write without all the emergency school runs and babysitting.

My own family, Ben, Sam, Amy, and Jago, are also trip-the-light fantastic. Ben never complains when I take off to festivals or on tours (or drag him to the ballet); Sam is my teen guru; and Amy and Jago let me waltz them around the kitchen on a daily basis, which always makes me smile.

I am deeply indebted to three wonderful women from the Irish ballet world who all helped to make Claire's story come alive — Harriet Parsons, Rachel Goode, and Monica Loughman, the original "Irish Ballerina." Harriet told me about her ballet journey a long time ago, and I've held it in my head and in my heart all this time. Rachel and Monica gave up some of their very precious time to answer lots of dance-related questions. Thank you all so much for your valuable help. Any ballet-related mistakes are entirely my own!

There is no company called the Budapest Ballet, and Claire's Budapest Dance Academy is also fictional, but the dancers from the real Hungarian Ballet and their talent, passion, and dedication were a huge inspiration. I was lucky enough to see them perform in the wonderful Budapest Opera House, and thanks to all at Brody House in Budapest, especially Will, for a magical visit. For photos of this very special research trip, see www.askamygreen.com.

As always, I have to thank my dear friends Tanya, Andrew, and Nicky, who have seen their fair share of my (real) dancing over the years, God love them; and of course my fabulous writer friend Martina "Zuma" Devlin; and quick-stepping friends in children's books: Judi Curtin, Oisin McGann, Marita Conlon-McKenna, David Maybury, David O'Callaghan, and Tom Donegan. And finally, Kim Harte and all the fab children's booksellers in Dubray Books. Booksellers rock!

My agents, Philippa Milnes-Smith and Peta Nightingale, are always in step beside me; and Mags and crew at Children's Books Ireland (CBI) choreograph fantastic book events on a daily basis.

When the Walker gang danced into my life, I was one lucky girl. Huge thanks to Gill Evans and Annalie Grainger for sculpting my every step into shape. Annalie was so dedicated to the cause that she traveled all the way to Budapest to check out the city for herself. She's a true Amy Greenster and knows Amy and Clover almost as well as I do at this stage. Thanks also to the lovely Jo Humphreys-Davies and Jane Harris for supporting the lifts; Sean, Hanna, Molly, Heidi, and the sales and marketing gang for making sweet music (about the book); and Katie, Nicola, and Sarah Coleman, who were in charge of the cover. And a lovely job they did too — I adore my new look. And finally, Conor Hackett is my leading man in Ireland, a great friend in books and a true gentleman.

I must mention my forever-young editor and fount of all knowledge Kate Gordon. Kate has been part of the Amy Green team right from the start. And a big thanks to the Young Editors who worked on this book with me and gave me such fantastic feedback, Yazmin de Barra and Anna Aldridge. It's a better book because of you, girls. I hope my next Young Editors do half as good a job as you did! (Look out for the next Young Editor Competition on the Amy Green website.)

And a big shout-out to three Amy Greensters, Rachael Mehak D'Silva, Mary Olabanji, and her best friend, Jessica Habenicht, because I promised. And also to the girls at Saint Catherine's in Rush, especially Leah and Kellie. Thanks for reading the books and for your lovely e-mails and letters, girls.

And finally to YOU, my dear reader. Thank you so much for all your e-mails, letters, cards, and photos. It's YOU who make the writing worthwhile. I thank you, Amy thanks you, Clover thanks you, Seth blows you a big kiss, and Claire does a big curtsy for you . . .

Please do drop me a line. I love hearing from Amy Green fans. My e-mail is sarah@askamygreen.com. Or check out the Ask Amy Green fan page on Facebook, www.facebook.com/askamygreen.

All my ballet best,
Sarah XXX